CITY LIGHTS

J. MORGAN

Copyright © 2014 by Julie Morgan

ISBN-13: 978-0-9913482-5-1

Edited by Rebecca Cartee

❀ Created with Vellum

ACKNOWLEDGMENTS

My girls Michelle Schwartz, Gretchen Purgason, Amanda Miller, and Tara Pennington, thank you so much for helping bring Blaine's story alive! Your feedback, humor and much needed commentary helped me out in so many ways. Thank you for everything you did for this story, for Blaine and for helping me keep my sanity while writing his story.

My amazing BETA TEAM! Thank you so much for cheering on Blaine's story, knowing he can't be all THAT bad, and loving him as much as I do.

Rebecca – Thank you for your mad editing skills and the commentary. I know some of this was very dear to your heart. Thank you for expressing as much. I love you.

My family and friends that have supported me through this endeavor. This story is very deep and touches on subjects that are true to life. Thank you for allowing me to pick your brains and bring a story of addiction and recovery to life.

To my husband John – Thank you for the many nights away and listening to me when I needed to run ideas by you, even those that you were not comfortable with. Thank you for being my rock when I needed your shoulder. I love you to the moon and back.

For my Uncle Johnny...may you find peace.

PROLOGUE

I don't like being out of control. I don't like not having everything around me... my way. Addiction... that's what they say I have. They tell me it'll all be okay. They tell me that soon, this too shall pass. What the fuck does that even mean?

Lexi left me. She was my life before my music career. I fucked her over, fucked my bandmates over... might as well hand over my contract to Chuck, my manager.

"Kid, you royally fucked up," he told me. He stood there, shaking his head like I should have known better.

"Don't fucking judge me, you fat prick! You have no idea what I've been through. You have no idea how this fucking feels."

Of course, this was one month into rehab. This was the morning I finally got out of bed, made my way to the bathroom, and found a stranger looking at me in the mirror. His eyes were sunken in and bloodshot. With his shaven head, honestly, he looked strung out. Who the fuck was this person?

Oh right, that's me. They told me this would not be fun. They told me I needed to clean up and get sober.

"The amount of drugs we found in your system... Blaine, it's a miracle you didn't overdose permanently," the doctor told me.

What the hell does he know? He's here to treat me. He knows nothing of addiction.

I bent over and grabbed the sink when my stomach suddenly lurched. Dry heaving first thing in the morning is something I'm used to. After an all-night binge fest on coke, ecstasy, and more liquor than I could hold… repercussions usually met up with me the next day.

Having rinsed out my mouth, the water dripped from my chin back into the sink. Small little fingers danced their way up my back, to my shoulders. They latched on and a faint whisper sounded in my ear.

Make the call. They'll bring you something, the voice told me.

My conscience enjoyed mind fucking me from time to time. "No," I told myself. My head began to pound and sweat beaded on my brow. I retched again then fell to my knees. I coughed a few times and memories of Lexi, my mom, and the band all hovered over me.

Blaine, stop it, please.

Why are you doing this? What happened?

Where did this come from? Who gave you this?

What did I ever do to deserve this from you? I'm your mother, for Christ's sake!

All these voices in my head fuck with me as my mind whispers its wants and needs. Just one more hit. Just one. One won't hurt me. It'll take the edge off.

I crept along the floor toward the bathroom door. My fingers barely wrapped around the edge of it and I pulled it open. My orderly stood outside, keeping some sort of guard. Guard of what? Who the hell knows?

"Help…" my voice was soft and it sounded rough. He looked down… all 250 pounds of former wrestler… maybe football player… turned orderly. He shot up an eyebrow and stared me down.

"Feeling better there, Mister Rock Star?" He squatted down

and his brown eyes bore into mine. This man, whose tag read Stanley, obviously gave no fucks about me, if the smirk on his lips was any evidence of that anyway. "I see your kind here day in and day out. Poor little rock star got his feelings hurt so he turned to drugs. Did someone hurt you before, Blaine, or are you lashing out at your upbringing? Did mommy and daddy mistreat you?"

"Fuck you!" I managed to mumble out.

"Ahh, so he lives." Stanley stood and shook his head. "Are you thinking, maybe, of trying to escape? Tell you what," he looked up and down the hall way for a moment then turned his attention back to me. He bent over and grabbed my shoulders, hauling me to my feet. He wasn't gentle about it and if I wasn't so fucked up on coming clean, I'd have fucking punched his nose in. "I'll help you escape and get some dope IF…" he trailed off with that same smirk, "you can get past me." He tossed me back into my bathroom. My back hit the sink and I fell onto my ass, hard.

"What the fuck, man?" I rubbed my back and stared up at the orderly. I sighed and watched as he crossed his thick arms over his chest. He's fucking with me. He's mind fucking me. Hell, he's probably in my mind right now doing this.

I looked away from the man named Stanley and laid down on my side, the cool tile chilling my sweaty body. The odd thing about going through withdrawal is the overly hot feeling your body gains during the process… but the cold chills. It's like having the flu. You're cold and shivering, yet you have a temperature.

Stanley turned and left my vision, probably standing guard outside my door. How did I afford such luxury? Oh yeah, I'm a rock star.

I pulled myself to my hands and knees and made my way back into my bedroom. I crawled up onto my bed to lie down. I stared at the white walls that surrounded me. Each time I closed my eyes, the nightmare that is my life invaded my mind. If I kept my eyes open, I began to see shit that wasn't there.

Isn't there something they can give me? Like a sedative? Oh yeah, they can't. I'm in rehab.

I can recall exactly when this started for me. It was my third big show. I barely made it to the end on fumes. We had a show the following night and I was completely exhausted. The band we were opening for, their lead singer... what's his name... offered me coke. I could kick him in the fucking nuts now.

Soon, it was ecstasy for the ride it gave. Sometimes, it was acid for the trips. After the shows, we drank until we couldn't see. I had women at my disposal. I never slept alone. I would close my eyes and if I were just sober enough, Lexi would be in my vision. So I drank more. I smoked more. I snorted more.

Something wet touched my pillow but it wasn't sweat. I hadn't cried since I was a child. The pain I put my family through, Lexi and her mother... especially after her father died. And now my band. Why did I do this? Oh yeah, because I'm an asshole, mother-fucker who only thinks of himself.

Well, that changes now. No longer will I allow the demons to control my every move. No longer will I allow anyone around me who uses. No longer will I allow any of this to control me. Never again.

But just one more time won't hurt you.

Fuck you, coke demons. Fuck you.

1

*M*y name was called; I stood up slowly and rubbed my palms on my jeans. Nerves spiked in my stomach, which I find odd because I'm the lead singer of a pretty famous rock band. I don't get stage fright when I sing. I don't understand how I can get stage fright when I face this room.

I kept my eyes downcast and mentally reviewed the notes in my head regarding what I wanted to say today. I gripped the podium and took a deep breath. Slowly, I looked up to the audience and exhaled. Eyes stared back at me from men that are in their early twenties to late forties, women that are young and older, slender and overweight. There are a few kids who stared back and for a moment, I'm back where I was when I was their age.

Their life is ahead of them and they had ended up here... of all places... I can attest, that it doesn't take much.

"Here Blaine, give this a shot." The lead singer of a band we opened for handed over a small, glass vial with white substance in it.

"What is this, man? This coke?" I couldn't take my eyes from the container between my fingers.

"Yeah, consider it a pick me up. Snort it. You'll get a fucking high

that will keep you going through the entire show... and then some." He *clapped my shoulder then walked past. "If you need more, come see me."*

"Alright, cool." I unscrewed the lid and looked inside. A small, silver spoon that looked like something Lexi would have used to feed Barbies as a child was inside. I pulled the small tool out and scooped the white powder on it. I sighed and realized how exhausted I felt. "Here's to new things." I brought it to my nose and snorted.

"Hello, my name is Blaine. I'm 745 days sober and clean." I paused for a moment and could see the calculations taking place in their mind. Two years is nothing to joke about when you're on your deathbed, dying. Everyone continued to stare at me. Some of the faces look blank, some look upset to be here, and then the younger girls in the crowd... they realized they were right; I'm THAT Blaine. They smile and grin to themselves. This is not what I wanted to happen today, but when you're the face of a rock band, it is what it is. They come here for help or they come here to say, "I did rehab with Blaine of Deep Ember! I got the shirt to prove it!"

"I've been asked to come back and speak, from time to time, as part of my rehab," *part of my penitence*, I thought to myself. "I'm here to let you know there is an end in sight and it is not through drug use. No one can tell you to just stop. You have to want it... need it. You have to be willing to accept the consequences for your actions, which for me, was very hard.

"I'm used to getting everything I want at the snap of my fingers. Anytime I needed a hit, a drink, or even to get laid, all I would have to do is ask for it." For effect, I snapped my fingers. "It was like having a genie, for all intents and purposes. Every day, there's not a moment I don't wish I could go back and change things. I destroyed a lot of people, ruined relationships," I briefly thought of Lexi and pushing her into Robert's arms... the douche. "I had no idea what it meant to love and care for myself. A part of me still doesn't, but I'm learning." I look at each person in the room and, as if all at once, they all visibly sigh and lower their gaze. Well, all except the groupies, who think they'll get some of me when this is over. "If you truly want this change, you will do it. Over two years clean and sober." I nodded a few times then stepped away from the podium. My palms were sweaty, but my nerves were calming.

Once the meeting was over, I ventured out into the lobby area and poured a cup of coffee. Bringing it to my lips, I cringed at the stale taste.

"Excuse me, Blaine?" a female voice asked from behind me. I turned to see who it was and found a few girls from the rehab session. They were smiling ear to ear, as if they had come backstage at a show.

Two were blonde and the other was a brunette. None of them could have been older than eighteen.

"Yes?" I asked them. I took another sip of coffee and cringed once more. "Horrible shit." I set the coffee on the table then crossed my arms over my chest.

"Wow," blonde number one whispered to herself. "Your arms are so... wow! They're big and I love your tats!"

I extended my arms and twisted them around a little to show what all I had. "Each one has a story. What can I do you ladies for today?" I asked them.

"Can we have your autograph?" blonde number two asked.

"Yeah sure, you got some paper?" I looked between the girls. The brunette brought her purse around, while blonde number one pulled her shirt down.

"You can sign my tits if you like. I'll have it tattooed on!" she smiled, obviously proud of herself.

She had amazing tits, she should be proud. I inhaled deep and tilted my head slightly as I stared at her cleavage, before I shook my head. "Sorry kiddo, can't do it. If you have some paper..."

She cut me off. "Kiddo? I'll have you know I'm... I'm twenty-one!"

"Sure you are," I started. "Now if you have some paper, I'll be happy to give you an autograph, but then I need to go."

"Where you headed?" blonde number two asked.

"Unlike you three, I'm not in rehab any longer. I'm actually going home. So paper?"

The brunette pulled out a small spiral notebook then produced a pen. She smiled and lightly chewed on her lip. She had an innocence about her that didn't seem to fit with her blonde friends. Not that it's my business to make assumptions anyway.

I signed three pages for them then handed the notebook back to the brunette. "Alright, y'all be safe and clean up. Take care of yourselves." I turned to walk away when I heard one of them whisper something about how I've changed.

"He would fuck anyone in his room. Now we can't get him to even look at our tits."

I shook my head and remembered my first experience with drugs, but I couldn't recall how I slid down the hill to shithead-ville. I had taken a lot of people with me and there were a lot of apologies to be made.

"All in due time," I told myself and got behind the wheel of my Mustang. It roared to life; I put it into gear and left the rehab center. I needed something new to focus my energy on. I needed something to pour myself into. I needed to remember who I am without the drugs. I needed my music and I needed to write.

~

I locked the front door to my house and leaned against it. Going to rehab was never on my top things to do each day. I hated going. It reminded me of who I was each time I walked through the door. Sweat would bead on my forehead and my stomach would tie in knots. Having survived my detox was bad enough; now I get to lecture those who were lost in their own mind... just like I was.

At first, it was court mandated that I do the rehab therapies. Now I do it because I want to. The people out there look up to me as an idol. I don't want to set the wrong example like I did before. I wanted to show the world I could be clean and sober. I needed this, if anything, just for myself.

I rubbed my palms into my eyes; the pressure took away the pain in my head for just the briefest of moments. I wanted more than anything to take a pain reliever, but a part of me worried it would become another addiction. I'm afraid to take anything for that reason.

"Fuck." My voice was a groan and a whisper. I pushed off my door and sighed. The entryway of my home was large with cathedral style ceilings. A large chandelier greeted me each time I came through. I wondered if one of the help would consider loosening it… allowing it to drop on my head. There were days I would welcome the relief of leaving this world.

I pulled my boots off and left them in the entryway. I hated dirt tracked inside my home. The cold of the tile seeped through my socks and it felt nice. I recalled summers in Texas when I would lie naked on the tile in the bathroom just for relief from the heat outside.

"Mr. Blaine, lunch is served," the sous chef in my kitchen called to me. The short, plump man was curt most days and never paid me much mind. I appreciated that more than he realized. People often thought being a rock star meant being an extrovert. In my case, they couldn't be more wrong.

Our band being signed was the beginning of the end for me. Stage fright used to plague me, but not so much now though. I needed something to get me over the hump. I needed something to relax me so I could have a good time. Smoking pot usually did that for me, that and a few shots of tequila. Half way through the show, I would get tired and the energy I had at first had been depleted. Again, I needed something to get me through… give me some much needed energy.

That was when I was introduced to cocaine. The high I gained was nothing like I had ever experienced. I lived for having coke in my body. Whether on a show or not, I snorted coke daily. It became part of my daily ritual. Wake up and take a piss. Brush my teeth. Snort coke. Write music. Sing in the studio. Snort coke. Go hang with the friends. Get drunk on tequila. Snort coke. I would sometimes do a line of coke off a woman's ass. Not one of my prouder moments.

I pushed the door open to the kitchen and stepped inside. The smell of Italian wedding soup filled my nose and I inhaled deeply. Chef knew I loved this soup. Why he continued to do anything for me, I had no idea. It's not as if I ever talked to him or treated him nicely. Hell, the man had found me sprawled out on the floor a few nights a week... sometimes in my own vomit.

A bowl sat beside the bubbling soup pot. I ladled some into the bowl then took a seat at the small table by the window. The glass was set up with one-way tint; I could see out but no one could see in. It was nice to have since fans and paparazzi would sometimes get into my yard and try to see inside.

My pocket buzzed as I sipped soup from my spoon. Pulling my phone from my pocket, a text from my manager, Chuck, lit up the screen. I swiped my finger across to unlock it.

Hey kid. We need to wrap up a few songs and get the next album going. Later. Chuck.

He always signed his texts. As if I didn't know it was him. I rolled my eyes and texted him back.

I have a few songs I'm working on for this album, maybe the next one, too. Be there in an hour.

I hit send and finished eating my soup.

I set the bowl in the sink then took the stairs two at a time up to the next floor. My study contained all my music memorabilia, my single platinum record from our first record and pictures taken while on tour. I ignored these images anymore as I poured myself into my music. If I looked at them, it only reminded me of who I had been, rather than who I am now. Always in a drug-induced haze, I don't recall half the shows I have done. It wouldn't surprise me if I stripped on stage. I was high enough.

I sighed, sat down in my chair, and picked up my guitar. I strummed it a few times, adjusting the tone until it balanced. I grabbed the sheet music I was working on and stared at the words.

"When I write, it takes me to a different place. I almost escape, as if I become a vessel and the words just flow," I told Lexi what seems like years ago now. Hell, it was. We were in high school. She was my first love and I totally fucked it up.

I took her virginity and her heart. I stomped on it like she hadn't meant anything to me. In a way, she hadn't. My first love was cocaine, then acid... sometimes ecstasy. The women I merely enjoyed fucking or sucking on my cock. Then somewhere down the line was Lexi. I didn't love her anymore, but I loved the idea of her wanting me... needing me.

"I'm a selfish son of a bitch," I told myself. "Who the hell holds a chick on a leash like that? Pieces of shit like me, that's who." I tossed my pencil at my music and sat there for a moment. I stared at the words and felt my eyes begin to burn. A tear slipped down my cheek and I quickly wiped it away. "Fucking pussy," I told myself. "Grow the fuck up."

Holding the chords in C, I strummed the guitar. The sound lit up the room in a way only a guitar can. I loved the acoustic sound. I loved it in a raw way, the only way music can sound intimate. Country singers play many songs this way but I couldn't stand the whiny shit that country music was. I loved my rock and roll. I loved the harsh aggressiveness of it. I loved the raw emotions it let out. Rock and roll is me, through and through.

Absentmindedly, I began to strum the chords to *Like a Stone* by Audioslave. This was one of my more favorite songs and if given permission, I would cover this on our next album.

> *On a cob web afternoon,*
> *In a room full of emptiness*
> *By a freeway I confess*
> *I was lost in the pages of a book full of death.*
> *Reading how we'll die alone.*
> *And if we're good we'll lay to rest,*
> *Anywhere we want to go.*

Music filled me... it completed me. It made me whole in a way nothing else could. My heart and soul were shattered glass. I needed to mend it back together. Somehow, I would, this much I knew. How or when was beyond me. Until then, I would simply give myself to my music. It helped block the demons tempting me to get high. Always a whisper, deep in my mind: *snort me, taste me, smoke me.* Not this time, not ever again if I could help it.

2

_I_ pulled into a parking space at the studio and sat in my car for a bit. The sun was out today and the weather was beautiful. Colorado was no joke when it came to summers. It's bloody hot and being this close to the sun will burn your ass in a mere second. Unfortunately, today I felt like shit. I've been clean and sober for two years, but not a day goes by that temptation doesn't show its face. Sometimes it is in the people I meet; sometimes it is my band. Most times, it is the person who stares back at me in the mirror.

"Well, the wicked don't wait for anyone." I got out of my car and headed inside. The cool air immediately replaced the heat from the sun once the door closed behind me. Chuck, our band manager, was on the other side of the glass wall. He looked up when he heard the door chime as it opened and shut.

"About damn time you got here," he grumbled. "We've been waiting on you." The glare in his eyes was not missed.

Chuck was a bit of a drama queen, at least that's what I've always told him. He babies us... well, babies me. He thought I'd fuck everything up being high all the time. I remember one of our last conversations like it was yesterday.

"Chuck, I'm fucking sober, man. Lay the hell off," I told him.

"Kid, you're stoned now," he retorted.

"Fuck off. I made us big getting in the news. Without me, you'd be nothing!" I turned my back to him and crossed my arms.

"No kid, we'll make it big, with or without you. The choice is yours. Be part of this or get the fuck out!"

His words are what did it for me. Be part of this or get the fuck out. That and almost dying. He was there when I checked into rehab and he was there to pick me up when I was released. Babying or not, the man truly cares about us.

"Sorry, man. I was writing music at home. You know, working," I told him with a lazy smile.

"Whatever, get in the booth. Your voice is needed."

By the time I finished recording, I felt like the entire day had passed. When I looked at the clock, I realized it had only been a few hours. I shook my head then ran my hand down my face. Right about now is when I would snort something; give me that boost I needed.

"Hey man, you alright?" Matt, our drummer, had walked into the room at some point. I never heard him. He's allowed his hair to grow out to his shoulders. His tall thick build took up the doorway to the studio. He stared at me like he was waiting on a time bomb to explode. In a way, I suppose I was that time bomb.

I nodded. "Yeah, fine. Just... sometimes it's hard, you know?"

"Honestly no, I have no idea. I had an uncle who had a drug addiction. I can remember him as a kid. He had the shakes all the time. Shit, watching him scarred me for life. I never wanted to end up like him."

A part of me wants to punch Matt for being such an asshole. I don't like being reminded how I acted, or possibly even how I was perceived. I know he's only mentioning this because, most likely, he has no idea what to say. Sometimes good enough should be left alone. If you have nothing nice to say, then shut the fuck up.

"Well, I never wanted to end up where I am... a spokesperson for fucking rehab, but here I am." I held my arms out as if presenting myself. "I never thought drugs would make their way in my path of least resistance but they did."

"Least resistance?" he asked.

"Yeah, least resistance." I smirked. "It fucked my life. All I can do now is move onward and upward."

"Yeah, I suppose," he offered. "You know the show we're checking out later?"

I nodded. "What about it?"

"You gonna be alright to go, I mean?" Matt rubbed the back of his neck and I could see him getting uncomfortable with this conversation. "If drugs make their way into the open... in your presence..."

Ahh, I could see where he's going with this. "I'll be fine," I told him. I lied my ass off because I knew if they were to make their presence known, the demons inside me would not stand idly by like they have been. I would go on auto-pilot and would wake up the next morning being forced to start over on day one.

"You don't lie well, you know that?" Matt grinned and shook his head. "I got your back, buddy."

I couldn't look at the man. Hell, I wouldn't be able to look myself in the mirror. Here I am, a speaker for the NA group, and I can't even be in the same room with coke. I knew I would use it. "I appreciate that man, more than you know." I sat there for a moment and dwelled in self-pity. When I looked up at Matt, I asked, "Why didn't anyone do an intervention with me?"

Matt chuckled, "What, are you serious?"

"Hell yeah I'm serious."

His grin shifted to a frown. "Well, to be honest, I don't think anyone realized your... umm... the addiction... was as bad as it was. At least not till..."

I cut him off. "Call it what it is. My addiction and yeah, it was a serious problem, especially when I overdosed in Texas." I shook my head. I almost died that night. The last person I expected to see was Lexi. The last thing I expected from her was forgiveness. I knew I had lost her completely that night. I almost lost myself.

"Well, you're back. You're better, but it didn't exactly help in the personality department." Matt smirked and shifted the weight on his feet.

"What the hell is that supposed to mean?"

"You're still an asshole."

I chuckled. "Glad to see you think of me as number one." I flipped him off. "Let's get outta here. I'm starving and we have a show to catch tonight."

~

e pulled up to the House of Blues in Boulder. We've played here a few times and the environment can be tricky, depending on the music played. Some bands rocked the place. Others just tanked. As a rock band, we were usually accepted. Once we were signed, people couldn't get enough of our music. Fans would sing along. Women would throw their bras up on stage, assuming their throw would make it that far. Then after the sets, groupies and band whores, as Chuck called them, would make their way backstage. It wasn't long until two or more were clinging to the idea of fucking me or sucking my dick. Hell, I looked forward to it.

I found myself staring at the illuminated letters outside the bar. I wanted to go in but it was like an invisible barrier was preventing me.

"You alright?" Matt asked me.

"No, but I will be." I sighed and stepped forward.

We walked inside the darkness of the bar and I could feel a cold sweat bead on my brow. *I can't do this*, I told myself. *Yes, you can. You kicked the habit. This is like cake. You hate the shit.*

"OH MY GOD, IT'S DEEP EMBER!" a female screamed at the top of her lungs. Immediately, like a frenzy, shit came unraveled.

"Chuck!" I yelled to our manager, "Get us the fuck outta here!"

"On it!" He yelled.

Chuck, along with a few security guards at the bar, made a make-shift barrier and we were, for lack of better words, shoved inside a holding area. The room was bright and the white walls didn't help with the adjustment of our pupils.

The smell of food filled my nose. So did the smell of alcohol. My mouth began to water and I thought for a moment, this is it. I'm done for; I'll fall off the wagon.

"So came to check out the competition, did you? Never thought I'd be in the same room with Deep Ember." a female voice interrupted my self-mutilating thoughts. I glanced up and did a double take immediately.

A slender frame, this petite woman stood before me with long, jet black hair. The side of her head was shaved and small patterns of stars, hearts, and diamonds were woven in. Her skin was pale and her light, sky blue eyes looked into mine. She was the most beautiful woman I had seen in a very long time.

"You must be Blaine," she said as she stepped closer toward me. She held out her hand and smiled. "Penelope Shade, or Penny Wise as I am called on stage."

"You named yourself after the clown in *IT*?" I asked as I shook her hand.

"He's my hero. He fucks with your mind. I love that shit." She grinned.

I couldn't help myself. I laughed and shook my head. "I see your target is not the children's audience then."

"Oh, hell no," she said with a grin.

"Right." I stared at her for a moment then, as a throat cleared, I finally lowered my gaze.

Chuck stepped forward and lightly grabbed my shoulder. "Deep Ember, meet Mongrels of Soul. Blaine, I see you've already met Penelope," he chuckled and continued, "She's the bass player and back up vocalist." I blinked as I watched her. It's not often we meet female bass players. I think I'm in love.

"This is Derek, the lead vocalist. He plays rhythm occasionally." Derek stepped forward, his long brown hair hanging to his mid-back. He was built thin and had tattoos that covered his arms like sleeves.

"What's up?" Derek nodded up to each of us.

"This is Scott. He's the lead guitar and back up vocalist," Chuck said. Scott had a shaved head and stood in only jeans. He had a piercing in his left brow, two in his bottom lip, a ring in his nose, his ears, and each nipple.

He grinned and waved to us. "Nice to meet you." His voice a deep bass.

"This is Joe, their drummer." Joe brought a hand up and waved, then took a seat in one of the chairs. His hands began tapping on the table in front of him to a song in his head. His blond hair was cut short. He had a few tats on his arms and he was quite strong, a far difference from Derek.

"Drummers are usually stronger than most members of the band. They hit shit for a living." I recalled the words from the first drummer I met when I was about fifteen.

"And this is Jordan. He plays the keyboards and rhythm guitar. He's also a backup vocalist." Jordan grinned and I think he blushed. Shy guy? I could relate. His build was tall and he was thin, like Derek. He looked European with olive skin and dark brown hair.

Chuck turned to face Deep Ember and one by one, introduced us as well. I couldn't keep my eyes off Penelope. She was beautiful. She was also a wise ass to call herself Penny Wise. I made a mental note to get to know her better. Chuck was looking to sign a new band under his label. I was interested in producing music for a new, up and coming band. Depending on their sound tonight, someone might get lucky and score both.

Maybe I'll get lucky and score with Penelope. I grinned and

felt my cock respond as well.

"It's about that time, boys and girls," Derek announced. He might be the self-proclaimed leader of their band, but if they sign with us tonight, that will definitely change. I noticed Derek staring at Matt, but didn't think too much of it. He grinned and made his way toward the stage entrance.

The opening band filed into the room after their set and almost froze when they saw us. I grinned and turned to face the other direction. I might be an introvert but the fact that Deep Ember is popular enough to get recognized makes me happy. It makes my head want to swell. It also makes me want to snort some coke.

My smile faltered and I took a seat at the table where the spread of food was set up. Fresh fruit and vegetables, chicken strips, french fries, cheese sticks, and quesadillas were set out for the taking. I munched on a chicken strip and kept my eyes on the table.

"Hey, you okay?" Matt took a seat next to me. He knew me better than most. He knew me too well and had been the first to come to the hospital when I was recovering. He never once threw it in my face or held it over my head.

I nodded. "Yeah, just old habits, you know?"

Matt nodded. "Penny is hot, huh?"

I turned in my seat to look at her across the room. She fidgeted with her skirt. The material barely covered her ass. Her see through shirt lay over what looked like a bathing suit top. The boots she wore were shiny leather that came to her mid-thigh. The woman was a goddess. "Fuck yeah, she is." As if on cue, Penelope looked up and caught us staring at her. She furrowed her brows and turned in the other direction.

"Mongrels of Soul," the House of Blues managers stepped in and looked around. "You're up."

"It's time to go play," Derek announced with a grin. He glanced over at Matt once more then he jumped up and down a few times in an effort to get his adrenaline pumping. Their lead guitarist, Scott, pushed him hard to the side and Derek stumbled. "What the fuck, man?"

"Quit jumping. You look like a damn fool." Scott laughed and walked out the door toward the stage. I laughed as well, so did Matt and Chuck.

Derek shoved Scott back and the guitarist grinned.

The door opened to the stage and the crowd was chanting MONGRELS! MONGRELS! MONGRELS!

I still remember my first set ever played and the adrenaline rush I received. The women screamed our band name and later, they screamed my name. I grinned at the memory then turned to Chuck. "Ready for this? It sounds like they have a fan base already."

He nodded. "They've done well for themselves so far. Their old manager, who was recently fired, did good to get them gigs but did nothing else to help them. He was charged with extortion and unfortunately, they'll never see that money again. No one would show them as much love as I would, so let's get this going."

Chuck was an asshole but he knew the business. When he says no one would love you as much as he does, he meant it. He would run you balls to the wall, but would be there to pick up the pieces if you fell. I would know; he covered for me a number of times before I was forced into rehab.

"I can find a new singer if you don't clean the fuck up!" Chuck yelled.

"You can't replace me! I'm the face of this band!" I told him in my drunken, high state of bliss.

"The fuck I can't. Try me, asshat! Pull this shit again and you're gone! I made you, I can fucking end you, understood?"

As much as he threatened, Chuck was there to pick up my pieces. I left a trail of shit and broken hearts everywhere we went. I had bogus calls that I had impregnated women and I left rooms in a hell of a mess; didn't matter, Chuck had my back.

ongrels of Soul began their first set. Their music was a mix of *Jimi Hendrix*, the blues, and hard rock all mixed together in what they call their soul music. Their sound was amazing. They came alive up on the stage. The crowd cheered the band on and, in return, Mongrels of Soul fed off the energy in the room.

Penelope was wicked on her bass. She took no prisoners when it came to her playing. She was a nice, polite young woman in the green room but here on stage, she was a lioness waiting to pounce on her prey. She was fucking hot!

I glanced over at Chuck and he grinned ear to ear. He knew he'd stumbled upon a diamond in the rough with Mongrels of Soul. Derek sang into the mic and the women in the audience melted.

"I heard he's been called liquid silk," Chuck told me.

"What the hell is liquid silk?" I asked.

"Fuck if I know, but if it's anything, I guess it's him."

"Am I liquid silk?" I grinned and when Chuck glanced at me, I batted my eyelashes.

He chuckled. "You fucking wish, kid. Women call you sex on a mic."

"Well, I like that better anyway." I leaned against the wall and watched the band play. Actually, I watched Penelope play. Her fingers struck the bass guitar like she was striking herself between her legs. Her head rolled back and her lips parted. She was the sexiest thing I've ever seen on stage. My cock told me so as well when it jumped to attention in my pants. Down boy.

Penelope glanced over to where Chuck and I were standing. She smiled at me then looked back out toward the audience. She made her way toward the edge of the stage and bent down, striking her bass in front of a few fans. They reached for her but they were just out of range. She blew a kiss toward the group and they ate it up. She was alive on the stage.

As the first set came to an end, the band members put down their instruments and headed toward the green room. Sweat covered and high on adrenaline, they came in panting slightly.

"Did you see that fucking crowd?" Derek yelled. The music made him a little deaf apparently. "Fucking A, man!"

Joe moved his arms around and flexed his hands, then relaxed them. "Great sound out there guys! Fucking awesome!"

Chuck stepped forward and I leaned against the wall inside the green room. He crossed his arms over his chest and his mere presence commanded attention. Chuck stood around six foot five. He was a wall of muscle and could easily pass as a bouncer in a bar. He shaved his head and had tattoos on his neck and arms. I teased him once about getting his head tatted up.

The band quieted down and turned their attention toward him. Penelope caught my gaze for a moment then looked at Chuck.

"Outstanding act guys, seriously," he started. "I love the sound and it's obvious the crowd loves you as well."

I pushed off the wall and stood next to my manager.

"Y'all know Blaine, obviously?" He motioned to me and I nodded again.

"Who doesn't?" Penelope retorted. I'm not sure if I was happy about her remark or offended. My brows furrowed and she winked at me. I decided to be happy that she knows about me but time will tell if it's because of my personality or because of my reputation.

"I'd like to formally offer a contract to you guys and get you signed." The group was quiet and it felt like all the air had been removed from the room.

I cleared my throat and took a step forward. "I'm taking a part in this venture as well. I'll be producing your music." I looked at Penelope and caught the surprised expression on her face. She lowered her gaze then looked at Derek. I wondered for a moment if Derek was not only the leader, but made the decisions for the band as well.

"How much are we talking?" Derek finally asked.

"All of that will be worked out in your record deal," Chuck told him. "I'll have my attorney present to answer any questions you may have."

Scott was the first to break the silence. "Well, hell YEAH!" He thrust his fist into the air and I almost choked on laughter. I remember when Deep Ember was signed and how it felt. I can appreciate his sentiments.

Derek eyed his lead guitarist for a moment, the looked back at Chuck. If he's trying to pull off the strong and silent type, he's doing a pissy job. Dude should be more excited. It's not as if he's *not* a dime a dozen. I caught myself on my own thoughts and glanced over at Chuck. He looked back at me and I held in a laugh.

"What the fuck is so funny?" He asked.

"Tell ya later, but I just had a moment of clarity on something you said." I patted his shoulder then turned my back on the band.

"What does it mean when you say you'll produce our music?" Penelope asked.

I turned back around and gazed at her for a moment. I could see excitement in her eyes along with fear. "Well, I'll oversee and manage the recordings in the studio. I'll come up with ideas on music to write along with your band, I'll assist in selecting songs for the albums, I'll be coaching each of you to make you better than you are now, I'll work in the control room as you record and basically, supervise everything."

"Will you wipe our asses, too?" Derek questioned. "I mean, will we have any control over what we'll record?"

"Attitude like that won't get you in the band, asshole," Chuck told him.

"Look, I meant no offense, but it seems like we're the puppets here," Derek stated. He glanced over at Matt then lowered his gaze.

"Go back out there and finish up your show," I offered, in an effort to break up the awkward moment. I looked at Matt, who just shrugged. "We'll meet over at my place tomorrow and meet with Chuck's attorney."

"Sounds great," Penelope offered. "Let's go back out there, guys!" She glanced over at me and I offered her a nod. She smiled and I felt something in my chest... like a flutter. I hadn't felt this since Lexi. I'm not sure yet if I'm in trouble with this woman or if an old part of me sees her as a conquest. For my own sake, I hope it's not the latter.

❧

The next day I met with Chuck at my house. We set up shop in my formal dining room at my table that seated eight. I don't use this room to dine in since it is just me here and occasionally, my band mates when we write or are getting ready to go on tour.

Papers regarding the contract for Mongrels of Soul were spread out on the table. Chuck's attorney, Leonard O'Neil, sat across from me. The tall, thin man looked to be in his late fifties with salt and pepper hair, trimmed beard in the same coloring and he wore a dark gray business suit. The man looked like he was all class, and as my former fuck buddy, Abby, would say, *"He looks like he just stepped off the runway."*

The doorbell rang; the band we were signing was due to show up any moment. I had given them directions last night before we left.

"I hope Derek's attitude changed," Chuck stated. "Oh, speaking of last night, what were you realizing last night? You mentioned something to me."

I stared at my manager for a moment as I tried to remember what he was talking about. "Oh, right. Well, singers are a dime a dozen. I thought about that last night when Derek was running his mouth and a moment of clarity hit me."

Chuck grinned. "I'm glad to see your head is in the game now, kid."

I couldn't stand it when he called me kid, but I had lost that fight back when he first signed me. He's maybe ten years older than I am but it didn't matter to Chuck. You could be twenty years his senior, he'd still call you kid.

The butler entered the room and cleared his throat. "Mongrels of Soul have arrived."

I stood and turned toward the entryway. Hell yeah, they've arrived and her name was Penelope. Good god, she was beautiful in the morning light. The absence of the stage make-up left her with an innocence about her. Derek, Scott, and the rest of the band fell in behind her and spread out through the dining room. Wearing old, tattered t-shirts and holey jeans, I grinned and welcomed them to my home.

"Feel free to take a seat. We'll get started right away." I motioned to the table and pulled out a seat for Penelope. She stared at me for a moment, then lowered her gaze. She made her way toward another chair and pulled it out instead. *Odd*, I thought.

I took my seat and glanced to Leonard to get started. He began by covering the contract details, how much the studio would take and how often they would be required to tour. It was all pretty simple, cut, and dry.

Derek reached for the contract and began reading it. I glanced over at Penelope and found her watching me. She immediately lowered her gaze to the table. I grinned and looked at Chuck. He nodded.

I think it took Deep Ember just a few hours to come to an agreement on a contract deal. We had a few questions and a few places were updated but other than that, we signed and were ready to go.

An hour and a few updates later, Mongrels of Soul signed with Chuck's record label. Everyone seemed quite pleased with the outcome. I shook everyone's hand in the band until I made my way to Penelope. A part of me wanted to pull her close, to feel her body against mine. I wanted to feel her ass in my hands, her breasts against my skin, her pussy in my mouth. Goddammit, this woman was sexy.

She offered her hand to me instead, and I took it. I brought it to my lips and kissed it softly. "It was a pleasure to do business with you today, Ms. Wise." I winked at her and she grinned.

"Cute." She removed her hand and took a step back. "I need to make a call. Excuse me." She stepped out of the room and I watched her ass the entire time as her jeans hugged tight against it.

"Blaine?" Derek's voice caught my attention and I turned to him. "So you have ideas on music?"

"Oh, hell yeah! Once you're settled upstairs we can definitely get started."

"Upstairs?" He asked.

"Sure. I have more than enough room for y'all to stay a while. No need to rush off." I wanted Penelope in my house, and if offering living space did that, this is what I wanted.

"Our home is not in Boulder, as you know," Derek offered.

"I know that, which is why I'm offering my home as yours. You don't have to stay here, but I thought it would be cheaper than staying in a hotel."

"Oh, well okay then." He looked at his bandmates who nodded in agreement. "Will the rest of your band be here as well?"

"Most likely just Matt, but yeah, they'll be in and out," I told him. Derek grinned and nodded.

"Makes sense to me," Scott said. "Thanks for having us."

A knock sounded at my door and Matt, my drummer, came walking in, not needing an introduction from the butler. He looked around the room and grinned when he saw Joe. "A drummer recognizes a drummer. Let's go, man; I'll show you the studio and where we set up to hit the skins."

Joe had a look of star struck for a moment, then he grinned. "Matt, right?"

"You know it. Let's go!" He clapped Joe on his back and the two took off.

Derek watched Matt as he left the dining room, then glanced back at me. "Where exactly is the studio?"

"Down in the basement, it is sound proofed and since it's basically underground, it's the perfect setting. Care to see it?"

"Hell yeah!" Derek smiled and for the first time, he seemed at ease with the decision to sign with Chuck's label.

I began to head down with the band when I heard Penelope's voice.

"No, we just signed; I'm very excited." She paused and I stepped around to watch her for a moment. Her back was to me. "No, I'm not sure when I'll be back. We're staying here at Blaine's. You know I wouldn't do that. Why in the hell would you even suggest it? You know I love you." My heart just sank at her words.

She has a boyfriend... or fiancé. "I'll call you when I can, okay?" She paused again and I saw her inhale deeply then release it. "Would you stop? He's not going to try that on me, okay? Besides, have a little trust in me that I wouldn't fuck him, alright?" My guess had been proven wrong; she does know me for my reputation. Outstanding. I grinned and thought, I could use this to my advantage... unless I wanted to gain her trust, if for no other reason than having her as a friend?

I sighed and tapped her on the shoulder. She jumped and quickly turned. Her eyes widened when she saw it was me.

I pointed to the basement door and whispered, "We'll be in the basement touring the studio when you're done."

She nodded and covered the phone. "I'll be a few more minutes. Thank you."

"You're welcome." I lowered my gaze and shoved my hands in my pockets. I slowly glanced back up then turned away from her and headed toward the stairs. I grasped the handle, looked back at her once more, and found her watching me. She looked a little frightened. Not sure if it's because she thought I overheard her or she was hopeful that I hadn't heard. Either way, I know she's off limits. I won't do to her what I did to Lexi. She deserves more than that. I may have been an asshole previously, but I refuse to be that person again.

4

_W_e make it through the first song and it was fairly easy. I waved for them to join me in the booth. One by one, Mongrels of Soul piled inside. Each person took a seat, leaving Penelope standing. I offered her my chair and she waved me off.

"I'll stand, thanks." She smiled and quickly averted her gaze.

"Right here, woman." Derek patted his lap. Scott slapped the back of his head and I held in a chuckle.

"What the fuck, man?" Derek asked and rubbed his head.

"Alright if y'all are ready, here's your first recording." I pressed play and turned toward the band. This was my first production and I think I was more nervous than they had been while recording. I needed to calm myself. I needed to relax. I looked around the room at everyone and watched their apparently happy expressions; everyone, that is, except Penelope.

She casually bit her lip and closed her eyes. Her fingers moved to her side as if she were playing an air guitar. Her head bobbed with the beat of the song. She was beautiful. I smiled, watching her and it was right about this time she opened her eyes. She blinked and the corner of my lips pulled up. I lowered my gaze and waited for the song to end.

"When will the drums be put in?" Derek asked.

"That's next. Are we happy so far?"

"Fuck yeah," Derek yelled. "Let's do some more!"

I chuckled and looked over at Chuck with a raised brow.

"Joe is in the other sound booth recording the drums to this beat," Chuck announced. "Want to walk over and listen?"

"Can we?" Penelope asked.

"You sure can," I offered. She smiled softly and looked at Chuck. He motioned for the group to follow him. As everyone began leaving the room, I reached out and took Penelope by the arm. She stopped and kept her gaze on the ground.

"I'm not going to try anything, just so you know."

She sighed and glanced sideways to me. "You did hear me, didn't you?"

"I wasn't planning on it. I came around the corner to find you. I'm sorry."

She shook her head. "Don't be. You did nothing wrong."

I nodded then released her arm. "Is he happy with you being here?" I knew I might be crossing the line with my question. She raised her brows in surprise at my question. Yep, crossed the line. "I'm only asking so whatever is happening between you two doesn't affect your groove."

"My groove is just fine, thank you," she told me.

"Hell yeah, it is. Your groove is sexy as hell." I grinned. She shook her head and smiled. "You're beautiful and from what I've seen so far, you seem kind. Don't allow a douchebag to walk all over you."

"Oh and you're the expert on all things douchebag?" She rolled her eyes. "I'll have you know…"

I cut her off. "Actually, I am. I wrote the book on being a fucking douchebag. One douche recognizes another."

"He's not a douchebag," she told me through gritted teeth.

I held my arms up in surrender and took a step back. "I wasn't trying to imply anything."

"Sure you weren't." She crossed her arms over her chest. "Are we done here?"

"Only if you're happy with him, then yes, we're done here."

"What?" she asked, obviously taken aback. "What is that supposed to mean?"

"When you're happy it reflects in your work. When you're sad, pissed, or upset, that also reflects. I'm producing you. I want you so fucking happy you could shit rainbows."

She snorted and covered her lips with her hand. "Well okay, I'm not going to shit rainbows or anything, but yeah, I'm happy enough."

I nodded. "Alright then, after you." I held my arm out for her. She did a curtsey and held out an imaginary dress. I chuckled and shook my head.

Joe was hitting the skins hard and he looked like he was enjoying himself, if the smile on his face was any indication. He ran through a few skits as he played.

"Are we keeping that in the song?" Derek asked. "I'm not sure it really works."

"We'll listen to it later and see what can be cut and what can be used," Chuck told him. Derek nodded and took a seat.

Joe came to an end and removed his headphones. He grinned through the glass and waved with his sticks in hand. He pretended to aim one at Penelope and tossed it. She giggled and shook her head. Comradery between mates is a necessity. I wondered how much Derek had with his band. I also wondered if I still had this with my own band.

I had pulled my shithead stunts in the past and they had stuck by my side. Then again, they were under contract with me; they may have not had a choice. If there had been a choice in any of it, it would have been up to Chuck. I sighed and glanced at my manager and grinned.

"What the fuck, kid? You fart?" Chuck asked.

I chuckled and everyone turned toward me. "Why? Because I'm smiling you think I freshened the air? I'm happy and I'm shitting rainbows." I glanced over at Penelope and winked. She grinned and turned back toward the recording room.

Chuck laughed and clapped me on the back. "Good enough. Alright, take five, Joe. Rest of you, back in the room. We have more shit to cover."

～

*L*ater that afternoon, I made my way to the kitchen to find a snack. I located a bag of corn chips and some salsa. I took them and headed toward the kitchen nook. It was located by a bay window just outside the cooking area. I've gotten a lot of my thoughts done in this spot. The sun would rise on this side of the house and the light it gave was perfect for writing music. Apparently, I'm not the only one who thought so.

Penelope sat in my usual spot. She was scribbling on a notepad when I approach. I cleared my throat; she set her pencil down and looked up.

"Oh, you brought snacks? Perfect!" She reached out and made grabby hands. I grinned and handed her the bag of chips. She pulled it open as I took a seat across from her. I twisted off the jar of salsa and set it down. "So, no New York City salsa?" She dipped a chip in the salsa then took a bite.

"Huh?" I asked.

"You know, the silly commercials about New York City? Get a rope?" She waved it off. "Never mind."

"Oh, the Pace salsa commercials?"

"Yeah. Never mind. It was stupid." She shook her head.

"So, what are you working on?" I asked.

"Nothing really, I'm just writing some thoughts down. I get my best work done when I'm alone." She glanced up and smiled. "So, get lost."

I raised a brow. "Excuse me?"

"Go away. You're distracting me."

"Is that good or bad?" I asked her with a grin. I ate a chip and waited for her answer. She only watched me for a few minutes. She raised a brow and continued to stare. "Oh, I can sit here all day and stare at you. I have no issue with that."

She sighed and lowered her gaze. "I do," she mumbled.

"Why? Do I bother you? Aggravate you?" I leaned in playfully and waggled my brows. "Turn you on?"

"No, you're starting to, and HELL to the NO!" She shook her head and made a shooing motion with her hands. "Now go!"

I chuckled. "This is the best place in the house to write. Most days, it's quiet." I winked at her. "I'll leave you to it then." I stood then stopped myself. "Have you considered taking the lead on a few songs for the next album?"

"Derek wouldn't like that, to be honest," she said then shrugged. "He's made it clear he's the leader and the lead vocalist."

I crossed my arms over my chest. "You realize that he's no longer in charge of that?"

She nodded. "Yeah, I know that."

"Okay, well I'm telling you, as your producer, that I think you should take the lead on a few songs. If he doesn't like it," I shrugged, "we'll fix the problem."

"What do you mean, you'll fix it?"

I sighed once again and lowered my gaze. "When I became a real shit to Chuck, he threatened me. Lead singers... the face of a band," I smiled looking at her and gestured to my face, "can be easily replaced. I didn't believe him. It took me seriously hurting him and myself to realize he was right." I lowered my gaze again and pursed my lips for a moment. I lifted just my eyes to her. "Think it over." She nodded then looked down at her notepad. "Your voice reminds me of Fiona Apple."

"Seriously?" she smiled as she asked. "That is like... fucking huge."

I nodded. "She has an amazing voice. So do you." I turned my back to her and started to leave the kitchen.

"Blaine?" she called.

I stopped and glanced back at her over my shoulder. "Yeah?"

"Thank you." I nodded at her and smiled. "Maybe you can look at the music I'm writing, see if it's worth recording."

"Right now?" I asked.

"What? Oh no, not now, but maybe another time?"

I nodded again. "You bet." I lowered my gaze and left the kitchen, leaving the chips and salsa in the care of Penelope. If small steps is what I needed to do to gain her trust, then small steps is what I would do.

As soon as I was out of the kitchen I pulled out my phone and sent a message to Matt.

Hey man. You busy later? Stop by. Mongrels of Soul are here and we've recorded their first song. The music is sick! Later.

I pressed send and pocketed my phone when Derek walked into the room. He stared at me for a moment and I raised my brows. He looked troubled, like he wanted to say something, but wasn't sure how.

"What's up?" I asked.

"Something going on between you and Penelope?"

I was caught off guard, not expecting this... of all questions. "No, why? Even if there was, it wouldn't be your place or business to ask."

"She's in my band, so yeah, it is my business."

I saw where this is going. He's either being territorial or he has a secret crush on the girl. Hell, probably both. "According to the contract you signed, she's in MY band now, Derek. You want to remain in it I suggest you get your shit straight."

"Is that a threat? Coming from the great drug lord himself, Blaine?" He snorted and shook his head.

"Get the fuck out." I stood my ground and stared him in the eyes. "Now!"

"No, I'm not going anywhere. It's my band, not yours. Furthermore, Penelope is not up for…"

"Penelope is what?" Her voice sounded next to us and I shut up immediately. I glanced at her and saw her eyeing Derek. "Penelope what?" she asked again.

"It's nothing," Derek said and continued to glare at me.

"You fucking heard me, dickhead. Get the fuck out!"

"Wait, why is he leaving?" Penelope stepped farther into the room and walked over next to Derek. "Did something happen?" She looked up at him. He nodded a few times.

"Yeah, our new business *partner*," he enunciated the words, "thinks he has a leg to stand on when it comes to our band. He wants to make a move on you and I told him to cut the shit."

"He what?" Penelope looked at me and I laughed.

"You know as well as I do that is not how it went down." I stepped closer and felt my hands turn to fists. "He asked if there's something going on between us. Hell, I didn't get a chance to answer his question before he told me you're off limits."

"I'm no one's property." She shoved Derek and walked out of the room. "I'm definitely not YOUR property to bargain with!"

I wasn't sure if she was referring to me or Derek but I'll go with the latter for now. "Take a walk outside. You pull that shit again; I'll have Chuck renege on his contract. You would do good to remember where you are. You're under my roof, Derek. You don't like it? Hit the fucking road."

Right about then, Chuck walked into the room, Penelope right behind him. "What the fuck are you two nut-bags arguing about?"

I raised a brow and glared at Derek. "Go ahead. Tell him how I threatened you. Tell him how much of a drug lord you accused me of being. Go ahead."

"What in the fuck?" Chuck asked.

"Doofus here came in from the studio and found me in here, right in this spot. He asked me what is going on between me and Penelope. I told him nothing, and if there was something, it is not his place or business to ask." I shrugged. "He thought otherwise because he thinks she's his property or some shit."

Penelope gasped. "You did WHAT?" she glared at Derek. "I told you I have a boyfriend. Blaine knows I have a boyfriend. He's not tried to make any moves on me! Hell, he offered to write music WITH me! Do you not want success for our band? What the fucking hell, Derek?"

Her face was turning red. Damn she was hot when she was angry. Damn adorable, too.

"I thought he was only coming after you, okay? He'll probably replace me with a better version of me anyway!"

"With that shithead attitude I most certainly will," Chuck informed him. "You need to understand, kid, that I manage your ass. He," Chuck pointed to me, "is producing your ass. You want to be big? You want to sell music? Listen to me and listen to Blaine's instructions. This is the ONLY time I will EVER have this conversation with you. Do you understand?"

"But Chuck," Derek whined.

The fucker is seriously whining?

"NO BUTS! DO YOU UNDERSTAND?" Chuck's face turned red and I thought he might have a stroke. Derek nodded. "You didn't answer me, kid."

"Yes, I understand," he mumbled.

"Good. You pull that shit again you're out of here." Chuck turned toward me and glared for a moment. "No fucking with the band members. That includes in your bed. Got it?"

I chuckled and shook my head. "I don't plan on fucking any of them. I don't swing that way. But if Penelope happens to find herself in MY bed, well that's a different ball game."

Penelope gasped and her eyes went wide. Chuck looked at her, then back at me. "Yeah, good luck with that fantasy, fuck-nut." He laughed and walked out of the room.

I shook my head and smiled. I glanced at Penelope and tilted my head. "What? I'm not planning to fuck you, unless you come to me begging for it." I winked. She groaned and stomped out of the room.

"Dude," Derek started then glanced at me.

"Don't," I told him. "Get your head on and know I'm here to help you." Derek nodded and lowered his gaze. "First thing you need to realize is, you may be the leader of your band, but here, I am. So is Chuck. What we say goes." Derek nodded. "That includes allowing Penelope to lead a few songs vocally."

Derek immediately shot me a look of disbelief. "But I'm lead vocalist."

"And she sings your ass out three days to Sunday."

"What does that mean?" he asked.

"It means, she's taking the lead on a few of the songs. Trust me. The fans will love her. So will you. You don't, there's the door."

Derek's face grew bitter but I could give a shit. "Whatever," he mumbled then walked back down to the recording room.

I stood there for a moment and waited. I knew she was listening. Hell I would be, too. "You can come out now."

Penelope peeked around the corner and looked at me. She had this mousy way about her that made her sexy in an innocent way. "Did you mean all that?"

"Did I mean all what, exactly?" I stepped closer toward her. Keeping a foot of distance between us, I leaned against the wall and crossed my arms over my chest.

"That I out sing Derek."

"I wasn't lying. You have a set of pipes on you that are freaking amazing. You need to be showcased."

"I don't know what to say." She lowered her gaze and stood there.

"'Thank you' works. So does 'ravage my body.'"

She immediately looked up, shock written on her face.

"Fuck woman, I'm kidding! I'm kidding. But hey, if that ever changes," I winked, "my room isn't too far from yours."

"You're intolerable!" She slapped my arm and stormed off back toward the kitchen.

"And you're a sex kitten!"

"No, I'm not!" she yelled back.

I chuckled. "Oh, hell yes you are," I said to myself in a lowered tone. I grinned and made my way back down to the studio.

a few days had passed since Mongrels moved into Casa de Blaine. We wrapped up another song and decided to call it a day. It was Friday night and we needed to get out of the house before a fight broke out. Too much testosterone kills the mood… anywhere. Not that we needed more chicks around here but damn, too much sizing each other up over who would do what when. Enough already!

"Alright, great set," I announced and clapped a few times. "Head upstairs and clean up. I'm taking out my new band for a night on the town! Drinks on Chuck!"

"What the fuck, kid?" Chuck glared at me. I chuckled.

"Okay, he'll split the cost with me. Y'all did real well." I glanced over at Penelope and motioned her over. "Can we talk?"

She nodded and set her bass down. She pulled a hair band from her pocket and pulled her hair back. She had recently taken the clippers to her head again and shaved the side. Someone had drawn in a few new patterns of wavy lines.

"Hey, nice update. Did you do this?" I asked as I motioned to her hair.

"Yep, sure did. All me. So what's up, boss?" she smiled.

"Ooh, don't call me that. If I ever take advantage of you, you could sue me for harassment." I grinned. She rolled her eyes. "Okay, in all seriousness, I've been working on some lyrics lately and I'd like to review them with you." I started to walk and invited her with me. "I'd like you to write it with me."

"Wow, really? I don't know what to say." She looked taken aback... maybe even shocked.

"Is it so hard to think I could write music?" I asked with a raised brow.

She laughed and shook her head. "No, it's not that."

"Then what is it?" I stopped and turned to face her. She chewed on her lip for a moment, looking innocent and almost adorable.

"Well? Can I be honest?" I nodded. "You're Blaine. Thee Blaine of Deep Ember. Why would you need my help writing a song? There's no offense intended, please know that."

I held my hands up. "None taken." I rested my hands on my hips for a moment and considered what she was feeling. "Does that intimidate you?"

She shrugged. "Maybe?"

"Well?" I rubbed the back of my neck and stood there, feeling a little off myself. This woman had definitely captured my attention in more ways than one. The way her doe eyes poured into mine, the way she nibbled on her lip when she was nervous, the way she lost herself when she played her bass.

I sighed and continued. "Try not to be, I guess. I mean, I'm just a guy who loves music. I'm pouring myself into it these days." I shrugged and raised a brow. "Call it my *new* addiction."

She smiled and lowered her gaze. "It's a good one to have, assuming there are 'good' addictions that is." She glanced up to me and held my gaze. "Okay, so what are you... I mean, we... writing about?"

I grinned and motioned for her to continue walking with me. "I want to write a song about finding love in the darkest part of one's self. Imagine falling into the blackest hole you can imagine, then suddenly this," I glanced over at her, "angel appears. She extends her arms down into the hole and pulls the guy out. She's his saving grace. She pulls him from the wreckage."

"Wow, that's beautiful." At some point, we stopped walking again. I'm not sure when, but we stood there and stared at one another.

Derek approached and cleared his throat. "Who's actually going to sing said love song?"

"Penelope is," I answered. Both of their eyes widened.

"So is she taking over the lead spot?" Derek asked. In all honestly, I expected malice from him on this, but what I least expected was genuine curiosity.

"Just on this song, for now. I want to showcase her voice. There's no reason the two of you can't both sing songs in the band." I felt like I held my breath for a moment. From the side view of my eye, I think Penelope was, too.

Derek nodded. "I think that's…" he looked at Penelope and grinned. "I think that's cool."

Penelope visibly sighed and smiled at her lead vocalist. "Thank you, Derek."

He winked at her then took the stairs up to the main floor, two at a time. "LOVE BITES, LOVE STINGS!" He began yelling the lyrics to Def Leppard's early nineties hit, *Love Bites*. I chuckled and shook my head.

"So you're good with leading on this one?" I asked her.

She nodded with a big smile. "Abso-fucking-lutely!"

I laughed. "That's my girl."

Her laugh toned down a bit and she lowered her gaze. "Thank you for this opportunity."

I touched her chin and lifted her face up. She kept her gaze to the side, not wanting to make eye contact. "Look at me."

She closed her eyes and took in a deep breath.

"Penelope, look at me."

She finally let out the breath she'd been holding and slowly shifted her gaze to mine. Her beautiful sky blue eyes were deep pools I could get lost in. I imagined for a brief moment, making love to this woman while I stared into her eyes, her legs wrapped around my waist while we kissed.

"You deserve this," I said in a lowered voice. "You are amazing and we need to get your voice out there."

She stared at me for a long moment without saying anything. She looked quickly at my lips, then back at my eyes. I slowly began to lean in, having courage from somewhere deep inside of me. That courage dared me to kiss this woman, to claim her lips. I wanted it. Every part of her body screamed that she wanted it.

Just a breaths distance away, her phone chimed in her pocket. She gasped and the moment was broken. I released her as she lowered her gaze. My hand grasped the back of my neck and I stood there for a moment, unsure what to do.

"I, umm... need to take this." She casually looked up at me. I nodded and pointed up the stairs.

"See you up there," I mumbled. She nodded as she pulled out her phone. I watched her for a moment then headed up the stairs.

What was I thinking? Were we going to kiss? Hell, I would have kissed her. I reached the top of the stairs and stood there for a moment. I closed my eyes and the image of her face penetrated my mind.

I imagined her gasping as I thrust into her, my hand lightly squeezing her neck... her naked body sweaty against mine. Holy fuck, I needed a cold shower.

∿

"*L*et's head on out!" Joe called from the front of the house. I walked into the front living area and chuckled.

"Got an itch you gotta scratch or what?"

He grinned. "Something like that." He had on his *Mongrels of*

Soul do it best t-shirt. It was a design he had put together a while back, or so he told me. His ratty jeans looked like they had seen better days; with the few safety pins he had holding his garments together.

"I'm ready." I turned at the sound of Penelope's voice. She stepped into the room, her hair pulled into a pony tail with ringlet curls. Her make-up was heavy but it suited her. The lining around her eyes made the light blue pop in an incredible way. The red lipstick made me want to have her lips around my cock. I wanted to grab her hair and watch her head bob up and down. The short black skirt with an over the bust corset perked her tits up that made my dick throb... I finally reached her stockings, connected to what looks like a garter under her skirt. Paired with black leather knee-high boots, fuck, she was going to make my night hard in more ways than one.

I felt my cock twitch and I forced myself to look away from her. I needed to turn around and adjust myself in my pants before we headed out. I don't need her... or anyone else seeing that I'm sporting fucking wood. Ahh hell, who cares? I reached down and adjusted my cock. Penelope's eyes widened.

"What? You made me fucking hard in that get up." I chuckled and grinned at her. Her face blushed a bright crimson.

"Should I go change?" she asked.

"Hell, no!" Joe and I said at the same time. We glanced at one another and Joe laughed. I grinned.

"Damn woman," Derek called when he walked into the room. "Your man know you're dressing like this? Fuck, he's a lucky bastard!"

Hell, yeah he is, I thought to myself.

"Umm..." She bit her lip and glanced around the room at the men eyeing her like candy.

"You look beautiful," I told her. She looked hotter than I'd ever seen her and hotter than any other woman I've ever been with. Damn, I wanted her.

43

We arrived at the club a short while later. Derek and Joe made their way to the bar while I stood with Chuck and Penelope off to the side. Jordan stood next to Chuck and gnawed on his nails.

"Dude, you hungry?" I asked and grinned. Jordan looked at me then at his fingers.

"Nervous habit," he said.

I nodded. "Understood. Just don't bleed on the keyboards." He grinned and shook his head. Jordan headed toward the bar. Derek turned and wrapped an arm around his keyboardist then introduced him to the woman next to him.

"Oh no," Penelope stated.

"Oh no?" I asked and looked to her.

"Jordan is shy. This could be something easy or something disastrous."

"How so?" I asked her. She tilted her head slightly and watched her band mates. My guys would have my back as my wing men if needed, especially Matt. It was nice to see she was this way with her guys as well. I wondered briefly how her boyfriend felt about it.

"Well? He could open up and be fun, or he could be so shy he runs, shuts down, and won't say anything. In which case, Derek takes the chick back to his," she paused and looked up to me, "his place?" She questioned her own statement and her brows rose.

"As long as they don't break shit and no one is sacrificed, I don't give a shit."

Penelope laughed. "Has that been an issue in the past? Sacrificial sex?"

I tapped my chin and looked to the ceiling playfully. I heard her laugh and when I looked back down, her smile lit up her face. "Not yet. Want to give it a go with me?" I winked and she shook her head.

"Not tonight, maybe another time." She smiled again and headed toward the bar. She stood on the other side of Jordan and whispered something to him. His eyes went wide and he quickly glanced at her. She winked and ordered a shot from the bartender. Derek looked between her and Jordan, obviously curious as to whatever she'd said. Hell, I was, too.

Penelope made her way back to me, putting a little sway in her ass. Jordan watched her the entire way with a lustful expression.

"What the fuck did you say to him?" I asked.

She shrugged and downed her shot. I had half a mind to lick her lips just to taste the drink she'd consumed. She beat me to it. Her tongue glided across her lower lip and it was all I could to just stare. I'm not sure, but I'm almost positive I groaned watching her. Chuck handed me a bottle of water. I brought it to my lips to take a drink.

"I told him to tell the girl he had his tongue surgically split so it would enhance the pussy eating experience."

I spit the water across the floor and Penelope took a step back. "You did what?" I asked.

She laughed and nodded. "You heard me."

"Did he seriously have that procedure done?" I asked and wiped off my mouth. I heard Chuck laughing next to me. I looked at him with a glare. "Next time, I'll aim for you, fucker." He clapped my back and crossed the floor to the bar.

"He most certainly did," she smiled and handed me her shot glass. "I'm going to go dance. I feel the need to give my boogie shoes a work out!" She turned and shimmied her way across the floor. The black lights of the bar caused anything white in her fabrics to glow. The laser lights that shot throughout the dance floor made their way across her body, tracing her outline.

I watched her for a bit. A part of me wanted to go out on the floor and pull her close, dance with her while her ass grinded against me. The other... hell, I just wanted to watch. She reminded me of a sex goddess who would masturbate in the corner while her lover watched.

I shook my head and decided on option three: walk away. I needed space and knew that since she had a boyfriend, she was off limits. I'd wanted to kiss her earlier and I think she would have let me. I sighed and looked at the bar. Derek, Jordan, and Chuck seemed to be having good time. Chuck glanced over at me and nodded with a grin.

The music became muffled when the bathroom door closed behind me. I heard a bit of a scuffle a few stalls over and I thought, very briefly, someone is getting high. I gritted my teeth and walked up to one of the urinals. I unzipped my pants and began to piss.

"Fuck, this shit is good," said a voice from the neighboring stall. He snorted and the door opened. I hit the button to flush and zipped my pants. I glanced over at him as he wiped his nose. That is when I began to feel the pull.

I closed my eyes and took a deep breath. When I opened them again, the other guy appeared and snorted the white substance from a small spoon. "Fuck me," I whispered. I stared at them for a long moment. The first guy, a tall skinny fucker with sunken eyes, glared at me.

"Got a problem?"

"Fuck, I need air," I said to myself. I shook my head and began to feel sweat bed on my forehead. I swallowed hard and stared at the small, glass vial in front of me.

The skinny guy grinned. "Wanna get high? It'll cost ya."

"How much?" The words left my lips before I realized I'd even spoken them.

"Fifty. It'll get you a few lines. A hundred and you can do it off my ass." He slapped his ass and I continued to stare at the vial.

I closed my eyes and held my breath. "I... I can't." Visualizing where the door was, I made my way toward it, intent not to look back. I needed to get out of here. I needed air.

You need to get high as fuck, my inner demon told me. *Once won't hurt you. Do it.*

"I can't," I told myself. I pushed my way out of the bathroom, followed by the two men who were snorting. The skinny fuck grabbed my shoulder and stopped me.

"You never saw us," he demanded.

"Get the fuck off me before I throat punch you." I turned and glared at the man. I might have seen red. He held his hands back in a surrendering motion and took a step back.

"It's all good, man. It's all good." He grinned and took off toward the open area. I heard him laugh and the sound was almost sinister.

I swallowed hard and stood there, then looked around the bar. Temptation was ever present and it teased at my mind. One line, one snort; it wouldn't hurt anyone. I could do this. I could do it once and get it over with. One taste is all I needed.

"No!" I yelled at myself and a few people turned to look at me.

"Hey, isn't that Blaine? From Deep Ember?"

Fantastic. Now if it wasn't bad enough having drugs in my way, now women would start pushing their way into my pants. If I could get high, I could fuck whoever I wanted. I wouldn't give a shit. I wouldn't feel anything. I would just be...

Penelope.

I looked over toward the dance floor, hoping to find her. Small glimpses of her body made their way through the crowd, like a lighthouse shining in through dark, heavy fog. She was my light; my haze was the fog. Fuck, I needed out of this place and needed it fast.

Hands began reaching for me, trying to grasp a hold of my body. I felt myself falling down that dark hole again and the hands in the crowd were pulling at me.

I made my way toward the bar where Chuck had been standing. In his place was my drummer and best friend, Matt. He was laughing at something and, as I stood there, he finally glanced over. His eyes went wide and the smile dropped. In its place was *Oh Shit.*

47

He saw it on my face, I knew he did. Matt came toward me and grabbed my arms. "What the fuck happened?"

"Get me outta here. Now." My voice was harsh and low.

"On it." He grabbed my inner elbow and pulled me through the ever-growing crowd. I heard Derek behind us asking what happened. I'm sure as shit that once his band finds out what went down, all will be lost. Outstanding. One moment of weakness and I fuck everything up.

We made it out the back door and the air outside was cool and crisp. It hit my body and temporarily shook me from the haze that had clouded my mind. I stared at the ground and felt my mind racing, trying to make sense of what just happened.

"What the fuck, man?" Matt asked me. "What happened in there?"

I glanced up at him and as I was about to speak, Penelope came running out. "Blaine? Holy shit, are you okay?"

I closed my eyes and turned away from her. I couldn't speak, couldn't say anything. I wanted her to know the new me, not the drug induced, fuck-as many-women-as-I-can, Blaine... the one she assumed was me. My hands gripped my head and I tugged on my hair. "I'll be fine." I lied to her through my fucking teeth.

"The hell you are! I saw the look on your face." She dared to step closer and touched my back. I visibly flinched.

"I think you should go back inside," Matt offered. His words were not harsh or mean, but they had a warning about them.

"I'll go back inside once I know he's okay." Penelope gently laid her hand on my shoulder and tugged. She pulled me around to face her. "Blaine," her voice was soft and low. "I'm here. Look at me."

I shook my head and held my breath. I felt afraid to breathe, felt afraid to feel anything, and knew if I did, I would indeed lose myself.

Her soft, gentle hands, fingertips calloused from thumping her bass and from years of playing, grasped my cheeks. She tilted my head up slightly. "Look at me."

I finally shifted my gaze to hers. Her eyes… those sky blue eyes, poured into mine. Her brows rose in concern as she held me in her hands. "What happened?" Matt moved to her side to watch me. Concern plagued his face. He's witnessed me, on many occasions, lash out, and lose myself to my own inner demons. I had serious anger issues when I let myself get out of control.

"When I went to take a piss, someone was snorting in the bathroom. I was alone and," I dropped my gaze, "it was the first time I've been around it since being clean. It's been a few years and in a moment, it all changed." I grabbed her hands and removed them from my face. Having turned my back to her and Matt, I looked up to the sky. "Temptation is the worst sin, outside of vanity. It showed its ugly face to me tonight… and I almost faltered. I didn't realize I had asked until I'd spoken the words, how much it would cost me." I turned to face them. "One of them offered to let me snort it off his ass, for fuck's sake."

"Do people really do that?" Penelope asked. I glared at her for a moment and she lowered her head. "I'm sorry."

"Take me home," I ordered. "I don't care who, someone get me the fuck out of here." I kept my eyes on her and Matt spoke up first.

"Here, take my keys. I'll get a ride back with Chuck." He handed his keys to Penelope. "You good to drive?"

"Hell yeah, I'm fine." She watched me for a moment as she clinched the keys in her palm. "Are you okay with me taking you back?" I nodded. She asked Matt where he'd parked and he gave her the directions.

A moment later, we were climbing inside. She turned on his Corvette and the air blew lightly. I reached and turned it on high. "Move your vents if it's too much. The cold air helps me." Penelope nodded and put the car into gear. It purred as she pressed the gas pedal.

"Are you okay?" She asked and glanced over at me as she pulled out on the main strip.

"Once I'm home and can calm myself, maybe take a cold shower, yeah then I'll be fine." I stared out the window. The scene raced past me as she drove.

"I'm proud of you, Blaine."

"What the fuck for?" I asked.

"You walked away. You could have succumbed and used, but you didn't. That's huge."

I knew she was right but I couldn't admit to it myself, at least not yet. When we pulled into the driveway, she turned off the car and faced me. "What do you need from me tonight?"

"I can't tell you that; you might slap me." I opened the door and got out, closing it behind me. She stood from the car and looked over the hood at me.

"I won't do that with you, Blaine, but if you need me to stay with you, just say the word. I'm yours."

I'm yours. The two words I've wanted to hear from her, but right now, in completely the wrong setting. I wanted... needed her to be mine. I needed her embrace, her comfort, and her arms around me. I needed to feel something familiar, something whole.

I made my way around the car and I stood in front of her. I held my hand out and she slipped hers into mine. She didn't question, she submitted. We walked to the garage door. I keyed in the numbers to open the door. The garage door came to life and lifted. I slowly looked at the woman next to me, the woman who was submitting to me tonight. She rested a hand on my chest and stood next to me.

Of all the things I could have expected, it wouldn't have been this. We only met what seemed like yesterday, yet, she was becoming so much more to me now than a just business partner. She was seeing my inner demons, she was seeing the real me. She was seeing me for who I was, not who I am today. Every moment of this broke my heart a little more. The more truth she saw of me, the farther away I knew I was to ever calling her my own.

We walked inside and I pressed the button for the garage to close. The cool air of the house welcomed us home. I kept my hand on hers, afraid if I let go, she would leave. I couldn't be alone, not tonight.

"Blaine," she began in a soft voice, "I need to change clothes. Come on, you can help me out of this corset."

I nodded and knew there was nothing sexual in her words. She could sense I needed her and could not be alone. At least that is what I told myself. She opened the door to her room and we stepped inside. She turned to face me and touched my face gently. "I need to grab a few pieces of clothing. Stay right here, okay?" I nodded. She slowly let go of my hand and stood there, long enough to know I was okay. This woman was a goddess and I knew in that moment, more than ever, that I did not deserve her.

She took a small step back and I watched her for a moment then lowered my gaze. She moved quickly, gathering her things in her arms. She unzipped her boots and quickly kicked them off. She unlatched her hose and skimmed them down her legs. I glanced up and watched her. Any other moment, I would be in heaven. Right now, I just needed her in my arms; I needed her comfort.

"Come on," Penelope slipped her hand back into mine and gripped it tightly. "Let's go to your room." She smiled and tugged at my arm. I followed her mechanically as we made our way down the hall. We reached my door and she waited for me to open it. I could only stare at her. She was beautiful; she was an angel who was watching me wrestle with my own inner demons. Whoever her boyfriend was, he was a lucky son of a bitch.

Penelope reached for the door and turned the knob. Pushing the door open we moved inside. She closed it then turned the latch, locking it. I wasn't sure why she did this at first, then realized, she didn't want anyone disturbing us… well disturbing me. There was no 'us'. After tonight, there never would be.

We left the lights off in the room; the moon shone in from outside, giving enough light to move around. She led me toward the bed and sat her things down. Reaching behind her, she tugged at her corset strings. "I'm going to turn around. I need you to loosen it for me. If you're not sure how…"

I interrupted her. "I got it. Turn around." She nodded and turned. She had a tattoo of a dragon that started on her upper shoulder and disappeared underneath her corset. "This is beautiful I told her as I examined the art work. She shivered so softly, I might have imagined it. I gently touched her back and allowed myself to feel her skin. It was almost like touching electricity. I was simply a tool and she was the source bringing me to life.

"Thank you." Penelope turned her head to glance back to me. "Blaine?" Her voice was soft. The moon reflected in her eyes and more than anything, I wanted to kiss her.

"I'm okay," I told her instead. I sighed and began tugging on her strings. Once it was loose enough, she began opening the corset and removed it from her body. Penelope's back was completely exposed to me. The tattoo made its way down her side, to her waist and disappeared, only to reappear as it peeked out on top of her skirt.

She grabbed her t-shirt and I saw a silhouette of her breasts. I closed my eyes and forced myself to turn around. Hearing her pulling her skirt off, then tugging on her shorts, drove me insane. The woman I wanted was practically naked in my room… and my back was turned.

Gentle hands touched my shoulders and she turned me to face her. She had taken her hair down and she smiled. "Get yourself ready for bed. I'm going to step in your bathroom to wash my face. I'll only be a moment. Okay?"

I nodded. She took my hands in hers and gave them a gentle squeeze. She let go then padded toward the bathroom. I sighed and reached above my head, yanking my shirt off. I tossed it and unbuckled my pants. I kicked off my shoes then pushed down my jeans. Left standing in my boxers, she came out of the bathroom, dabbing a hand towel on her face. She froze in front of me, her eyes wide.

"What is it?" I asked, fearful she has realized she was making a mistake staying with me.

She blinked and quickly lowered her gaze. "Umm... I didn't realize you were... umm..." She dropped the towel and shook her head. "You're in really good shape." She finally looked back up. Penelope smiled and shifted her weight to one foot. She covered her lips with her hand and in this moment, she was perfection. No make-up, simple, shy, and completely beautiful.

"Well, you're quite stunning yourself." I pulled my gaze away from her and turned to my bed. I pulled the covers down and sat. I faced her and wondered, *what now?*

I think she thought the same thing. She came to stand in front of me. I looked up at her and wanted to pull her closer. I wanted to feel her against me. I wanted to feel myself inside her.

She surprised me and stepped closer, without my help. She stood between my legs and wrapped her arms around my neck. She bent over and pulled me into a hug. Her dark ringlets fell around her shoulders then onto my chest. I closed my eyes and inhaled her scent; her vanilla soap and perfume invaded my nose.

I slowly moved my arms around her and hugged her back. My fingers dug into her skin slightly, pulling her closer. She turned her face into my neck. I could feel her lashes against my skin. "Are you okay now?" she whispered, her breath lightly touching my skin. She had no idea what she was doing to me or how she was making me feel.

"I'm... yeah, I'm okay."

She pulled back just enough to look into my eyes. "Do you need me to stay?" Her voice was a soft whisper.

"I would be lying if I said no."

She nodded then leaned in. I thought she was going to kiss me. Then her lips touched my cheek. "Lay down. I'll be right beside you. I promise; I won't leave until the morning." I moved my hands to her waist and held her there for a moment. If I turned to my left just slightly, we would kiss. I swallowed hard and hesitated. Just as I was about to face her, she pulled away.

I watched her as she walked around the bed, to the other side. She tugged the covers down and climbed inside. I couldn't help but smile at this beautiful creature next to me. "As much as I've wanted to get you in my bed, this was not one of the scenarios I had in mind."

She smiled and padded the mattress. "Let's get some sleep."

I lay down and turned on my side to face her. "Will you let me hold you?" She bit her lip and looked away. "I promise; I won't try anything. The closeness will help." She looked up at me then nodded. "Turn on your other side. That way I won't be tempted to kiss you."

I heard her gasp softly to herself. Penelope began to turn over and I wanted more than anything to push her on her back and climb on top. I wanted to make love to this woman. I wanted to claim her as mine. I also knew if I did this, I would ruin any chance at a true friendship with her. I needed her in my life, more than I had even realized.

Once her back was to me, I wrapped an arm around her slender frame and pulled her close to me. Spooning against her body, I moved my face closer to her shoulder. I lifted my head to look over her neck, shoulder and the length of her body. I wanted to kiss her neck. I wanted to grasp her breasts in my hands. I wanted to shove my fingers into her slick folds. I wanted to taste her on my tongue. Right now, what I wanted didn't matter. This beautiful creature in my arms had given herself to me tonight, freely, of her own accord. She opened herself to me in a way no one else had. She was my person. She was now my friend. No matter what, I wouldn't fuck this up. I wouldn't jeopardize her friendship.

I laid my head down and inhaled the scent of her shampoo. I tugged her just a bit closer. She nuzzled against my chest and rested her hand on top of mine, intertwining our fingers.

"Good night," she whispered.

"Good night, Penelope." I closed my eyes and allowed myself, for the first in what I hoped was many, a night of peaceful sleep.

---

6

*T*he morning sun warmed my face and I squinted. I wasn't ready to wake up. I had a beautiful woman in my dream and damn, her lips felt good around my cock. The dream continued to fade and I was left with the remains of a morning wood. I groaned and turned on my side. Hair tickled my nose and when I opened my eyes, for a brief second, I forgot Penelope was in my bed.

My heart pounded against my chest when last night suddenly crashed back inside my head.

Drugs.

Cocaine.

Temptation whispering in my ear.

I squeezed my eyes closed and willed the self-mutilating thoughts from my mind. I inhaled then slowly released it. When I opened my eyes once again, I looked over the body of the goddess in my bed, and appreciated her curves... much more than I should have. I relaxed into her and wrapped an arm around her body. My face buried itself in her neck. I felt her move against me. Her ass grinded against me, letting me know she wanted more.

"Mmm," she groaned to herself, "already? It's so early, Marcus."

"What?" I blinked and pulled away. Fuck, she thought I was her man. I closed my eyes and rolled onto my back.

Penelope quickly turned over and stared at me with wide eyes. "OH. MY. GOD." I glanced up at her and I tried hard, really hard, not to laugh. It got the better of me and I chuckled out loud. She frowned and her brows creased. "What the hell is so funny?"

I brought my fist to my mouth and bit down on my knuckle. I snorted and she rolled her eyes. "I'm sorry," I said as my voice cracked. "The look on your face!"

"What? The look of oh crap, I just grinded on my boss and thought, I don't know, briefly he was my boyfriend because he was all up in my shit?" She quickly got out of bed and stood there. She looked around and remembered where she'd left her clothes. Penelope marched around the room as she grabbed her garments.

"I'm glad you find this funny, Blaine. I most certainly do NOT!" She stomped her foot. I swear she got hotter the madder she became.

"Woman," I sat up and rested my bare back against the headboard. I watched her across the room as she held my gaze. "I was still dreaming and forgive me, she was hot!" I reached underneath the covers and adjusted the obvious wood I was sporting.

Her mouth dropped open and she quickly turned her back to me. "Who, exactly, were you dreaming about?"

"Isn't it obvious?" I asked. I threw the covers off me and got out of bed. I walked up behind her and whispered in her ear, "You."

She quickly turned to face me and almost jumped back. I guess my closeness to her was too much. I wouldn't have said those words last night. "Is it always like this with you? You become vulnerable and the first moment you can, you hide behind the tough exterior?"

I raised my brow. "You found me in a moment of weakness. Any other time, this is always me, babe. Take it or leave it." I held my arms out to the side and grinned.

Penelope groaned and headed toward the door. She grabbed the handle and jiggled it.

I walked up behind her and reached out, my lips next to her ear. "You locked it last night when we got inside." I unlocked it and turned the handle.

"Obviously, my mistake," she said. She pulled the door open and stood there. She looked back at me and sadness replaced the anger. "You don't have to hide behind this player exterior. I saw you last night, the real you." She lowered her gaze and she blinked. Her face began to blush and I realized she saw the erection in my boxers. I pressed my lips together to keep from grinning. "I liked what I saw in you last night, Blaine." She glanced back up at me again. "Stop hiding."

"No one is hiding," I said in a lowered voice. "Come back inside and I'll show you exactly who I am." I grinned and waggled my brows.

She groaned and immediately left my room. My grin dropped to a frown and I shut the door. Leaning against it, I slid down until my ass hit the floor. My head hung between my shoulders and I thought to myself, *way to fuck things up. You always push people away rather than letting them in. Hell it's a defense. Rather keep them at arms' length than allowing them to hurt me. Self-preservation at its best.*

Getting to my knees, I stood up and headed toward the bathroom. I needed a shower. Today would be a long day and I could only imagine the sneers I'd get from Penelope. At least I won't worry about hurting her. She thinks I'm a bastard... rightfully so.

Looking at myself in the mirror, I ran my hand down my face. The scruff was already a dark shade on my face. I sighed, turned on the shower, and then took a piss. Afterward, as I brushed my teeth, I recalled last night's events in the men's room... the drugs, the cocaine, and Penelope... What would I have done if the band had not been there? What if it had just been me? There's no way I would have left there sober. I'm a fucking joke, to myself, and anyone I try to convince otherwise.

The bathroom began filling with steam and I rinsed my mouth. All I needed now was for Penelope to run her mouth to her band mates on how bad I fucked up last night. Excellent start to a new business venture. "Let's go party and watch Blaine fuck himself," I said to the man in the mirror. I turned and stepped into the shower. The hot water singed my skin and I let it. It was a welcome relief from the pain of the thoughts about what could have happened that plagued my head.

∿

I pulled on an old, worn out t-shirt of mine from our first gig as Deep Ember. *Deep Ember World Tour 2004.* I can't believe this much time has passed since we first toured. What an adventure it was… what I remember of it, anyway. Hell, I was high or passed out most of the time. Chuck… always there to pick up the pieces. I owed that man a lot.

Making my way into the kitchen area, my cook was busy at the stove. He looked over at me and nodded. I grabbed his shoulder and gave it a squeeze as I walked past. He plated an omelet for me as I opened my fridge and pulled out some orange juice. When I closed the door, Penelope was on the other side. I jumped.

"Damn woman, you scared me." I grinned and held out the juice. "Want some?"

She shook her head. "When you're ready, come downstairs so we can talk."

"Anything you have to say, say it here. I need to eat, then I'll be down. We have songs to record. Then you and I have a date with some paper and a pen." I winked at her and took a bite of omelet.

She rolled her eyes. "You might fool everyone with this I'm a player and tough as shit act but you don't fool me, Blaine."

"I have no idea what you mean." I took another bite and

glanced over at her. She fucking saw right through me. She knew it. I knew it. I lowered my gaze and swallowed my food. For a moment, I thought it would lodge with the obvious lump in my throat. "Don't, okay?" I whispered.

"I never would." She reached over and squeezed my hand. "Just don't push people away when we want to help."

I nodded and looked back at her. "I'll be down in a bit," she smiled and leaned in. She kissed my cheek. Penelope slowly pulled away and looked into my eyes. "You're still a bastard. Maybe I'll upgrade you to son of a bitch soon." She winked and pulled away. I could only smile.

She walked out of the room wearing a fitted black t-shirt and skinny jeans. She had on her Doc Marten's, unlaced and comfortable on her feet. Her hair was pulled to the top of her head in a messy pony tail. She was the picture of perfection.

"She's beautiful," my chef mumbled.

"That she is…. that she is."

I made my way downstairs and everyone but Joe was already set up to record. He sat in the chair next to me and watched as guitars were strapped and mic checks were tested.

"So, what happened to you last night?" Joe asked.

"What?" I turned to him and he glanced over at me.

"You left us at the club. Did something happen?"

"Yeah, my attention was needed back here." I turned back to the band and turned on the sound. I pulled my mic close. "Alright, y'all ready?" They nodded and Penelope looked at me and smiled. I gave her a lopsided grin.

"Did that something happen to be our bassist?"

I sat back in my chair and switched off the mic. "Not that it is your concern, but no. I needed help back here and she offered hers. End of story." I looked over at him. "I respect her. I wouldn't take advantage of that."

"Alright," he sat back in his chair and relaxed. "Word has it you've been sober for a few years." He shrugged. "I thought maybe you fell off your wagon and she helped scrape your ass up."

"Dude, that's harsh words."

He looked over at me and raised a single brow. "Don't bullshit a bullshitter. If you're alright, I'll believe you. Just," he looked over at Penelope, "don't drag her into it. She's been through a lot. She's not as tough as she looks."

I glanced over at Penelope and watched as she tuned her bass. I had no idea what she'd been through; hell, I'd never asked. "Thanks Joe, I appreciate the words." I began turning up nobs and tested the recording device. "Truly, I mean that." I looked at him and nodded.

"Cool." The band started on their song and Joe tapped along to his own beat on his legs. His head bobbed to the music that roared through the recording studio.

We finished the song a few hours later. Recording, and recording, just to record one more time until it was perfect. Next was lacing in Joe's drums. The crew came into the sound booth and took a few seats. I began playing back the song, minus the drums. Everyone began to smile.

"Dude, we sound fucking awesome!" Derek exclaimed.

"Hell, yeah you do!" I told him.

A phone started ringing in the room. Penelope stood and pulled her phone from her pocket. "Umm guys, I'll be right back." She glanced at me then headed toward the stairs. I heard her answer, "hey baby" before she got to the top of the stairs. My heart sank just a little.

After we finished listening to the song three different times, it was time to set up Joe. He was stretching his arms and twirled his sticks a few times in his fingers.

"Whenever you're ready, dude," I announced through the mic. He nodded and pointed at me, giving me my cue.

He pulled his headphones on and closed his eyes. The man

became a machine behind the glass. Once he started hitting the skins, it was like he was having an out of body experience.

Joe pounded out the drums to the song in perfect harmony with Penelope's bass. My thoughts turned to her and when I looked around the room, I noticed she wasn't back yet. I turned my attention back to Joe as he continued to play.

"Derek," I turned to the lead vocalist. "Want to go check on Penny Wise? Make sure she's good?"

"Sure man." He stood and flashed up his index and small fingers to Joe, the symbolic rock and roll gesture. Joe opened his mouth and shook his head with his tongue out. I chuckled.

Derek headed out of the room as Joe wrapped up the song. "How was it, boss man?" He asked while pulling off the headphones.

I turned on the mic. "Come on inside so we can give it a listen once it's blended."

"Cool." He sat the sticks down and walked inside.

A few minutes later, Derek came back. He sat down and looked at me.

"Well?" I asked.

"Oh, she's fine. She's upstairs arguing with her boyfriend again. Seems he can't take the damn hint she's been signed and is part of a successful band. He doesn't want her around us and thinks she'll drop her pants at the first sign of a dick."

"Wow, that's a lot of trust he has in her, huh?" I was curious why he would not trust her and why she would put up with his shit.

"I don't ask and don't get involved. Just... fuck man, he gives her grief all the fucking time." Derek shook his head. "We all sort of took on the big brother role with her."

"I'm like a big brother but she's two years older than me," Jordan added. "She's a cool chick. She deserves better than that douche."

"Why does she put up with it?" I asked. I knew the answer but didn't want to admit it to myself.

"She loves him," Derek offered. "Or at least, she did love him. When he started accusing her of cheating, she would take it at first, but now, she tells him to drop the shit or she'll end it. For the most part, he will, and then he just starts it up again."

I nodded and kept my gaze down. I was a lot like that to Lexi. I cheated on her all the damn time, and kept her on a short leash. I was King of the Douchebags. "Well, let's continue splicing the song. It's about ready." I thought about Penelope. I thought about going up there and taking the phone from her. I thought about telling her boyfriend to fuck off and that she deserved better. I wasn't good for her and I knew it. She did deserved so much more. She deserved better than anything I could ever offer her. I knew that for damn sure. The pain of it hurt my head… and pulled at my chest.

I sighed and turned the track. The music filled the uncomfortable void in the room. "She'll figure out what she needs to do. 'Til then, just be her support like you've always been."

"Cool," Joe remarked. I glanced over him and chuckled.

"Do you know any other words?"

Derek laughed and Jordan coughed, spitting his water in his lap.

"Oh, damn, I'm sorry about that!" I laughed out. "There are towels in the cabinet over there." We tend to sweat while playing our instruments. Having towels handy is a must.

While Jordan cleaned himself up, Joe remarked, "Yeah, I know more words. I have an extensive vocab. Cool is only one of my words in my repertoire."

"I don't think I know that word," Derek said. We all looked at him then we began to chuckle. "What? What did I miss?"

Right about this time, Penelope came back down and her eyes were a little swollen and red from crying. I stood and stared at her. She wiped at her eyes and smiled to all of us. "I'm single now; I plan on staying that way. I had enough and broke it off."

"About fucking time," Derek told her.

Jordan stood and crossed the room. He pulled her in a hug. "You alright, kiddo?"

She smiled and let out a small laugh. "Last I checked I was older than you."

"Well, right now, you're like my little sister, alright?" He pulled her close again and hugged her. She nodded against his shoulder and sobbed once. "What happened?"

She sighed and pulled away. She looked me right in the eyes and I had a feeling I knew exactly why they broke up. Me. "He doesn't like me staying in the same house with Blaine. He thinks I'm going to *fuck him*." She air quoted around the words.

I lowered my gaze and sighed. The man wasn't too far from the truth. "I'm sorry," I offered.

"For what?" she asked. "For him being a senseless, spineless, dickless asshole? Okay, then I forgive you, not him."

I glanced up at her and looked into her eyes. The light blue color seemed a bit darker with her emotion. "For what it's worth, I am sorry he blamed me for how he was feeling." She nodded and wiped her eyes again.

Crossing the room, I grabbed one of the towels from the cabinet and unfolded it. I handed it over to her. The terrycloth material was soft. The material would feel nice against her skin... at least I hoped it would.

"Thank you," she whispered as she took the towel. She glanced up to meet my gaze then looked back down. She wiped her eyes then inhaled deeply, slowly letting the air out of her lungs. "Fuck him. Okay, let's record some epic shit! Later, we party!"

"Hell yeah!" Derek jumped from his seat and pulled her into a hug. "Best idea today!" she smiled and glanced at me.

"Let's get the music done first," I began, "then if we're not beat, we'll have a party here. How's that sound? I'll invite the rest of Deep Ember over and maybe we'll have a jam session."

"Cool," Joe offered. We all chuckled. Penelope kept her gaze on me and offered a soft smile. She was hurting. She needed a friend. I would do my best to be for her, what she had been for me last night.

I sighed and lowered my gaze. "Hey guys, I'll be right back." I turned to leave the room and headed up the stairs. Penelope was vulnerable. The last thing she needed was someone to take advantage of that. The last thing I wanted was to be her rebound guy.

I pulled out my phone and texted Matt.

Party tonight at my house. Bring the crew.

I pressed send and pulled up Chuck's name. Pressing call, I brought the phone to my ear.

He answered the phone. "What's up, kid?"

"Not much. We're having a get together tonight at my house, both bands. You should be here, you know, because you're such the cool guy and all." I grinned into the phone. He knew I was being a smartass.

"You're a fuck-tard, you know that?"

"Yep. You keep me honest. What can I say?"

He laughed into the phone. "If I'm making an appearance because I'm babysitting your ass, you got another thing coming."

Penelope came up out of the recording area. I turned to face her and gave a wink. "Damn, Chuck, it's not like that. You hurt me. You cut me deep just now." I pretended a knife had been shoved into my chest. I held onto the counter and made an awful face. She giggled to herself.

"Whatever. See you later, kid." Chuck hung up the phone. I stood straight and shoved my phone in my pocket.

"You have a beautiful smile. Don't allow anyone to take it from you." I walked over to her and stood there for a moment, unsure of where my friendship boundary stood with her.

Penelope lowered her gaze and offered a slight shrug. "Well, when one tells you that you're not worth it multiple times, one begins to believe it."

"You can't be serious?"

She lifted her gaze to me, her eyes wet with moisture again. Ahh hell, she's going to cry. I took a chance and opened my arms to her. Her bottom lip trembled when she stepped into my embrace. She hiccupped against my chest and my arms tightened around her.

"It'll take time, but you'll realize, soon enough, he's not worth it. If he loved you, he would know better than to say anything otherwise." I held her close and imagined the same words being repeated to Lexi. I shook my head. I was a real asshole to her.

"Th-thank you," she mumbled against my chest.

"Anytime, beautiful. Now listen to me," I touched her chin and lifted her face. Her swollen, red eyes looked up into mine. "What do you like to do for fun? Other than play your bass?"

She shrugged. "I'm not sure I even know anymore. I was with him for so long, and then being in this band, well it didn't leave room for much else."

I could certainly understand that. "Do you enjoy bikes? I have an extra helmet in the garage begging to be on top of a beautiful woman's head."

Penelope laughed. "You make helmets sound so exciting."

"Oh, but they are! Didn't you know?" I winked and she smiled. "How about a ride up to the mountains? Get some fresh air? I can take you up to one of the peaks and you can scream as loud as you want. No one will care. No one will be around to say shit."

"So," she began and stepped back from my embrace. She wiped at her eyes and gathered herself. "What you're saying is that you plan on taking me somewhere that if I screamed in terror, no one would hear me?"

I grinned. "You got it."

"Alright, I'm in," she smiled.

"Ahh, there it is."

She raised her brows. "There what is?"

"Your beautiful smile," I couldn't help it; I winked.

She lowered her gaze and shifted the weight of her feet. "Blaine, I…"

I stopped her before she could say anything else. "Don't, okay? I understand. It's only a ride, nothing more. A change of scenery will help."

She nodded and looked back up. "Thank you."

"You're welcome."

Penelope turned and left the room. The rest of the band came up from the studio. Derek stretched and yawned. Jordan pretended to punch him in the gut. I grinned at them and chuckled. Joe and Scott came up shortly after.

"Y'all decide to fornicate in my house tonight, it's cool, just don't break anything and for fucks sake, don't splooge on the wall, comforter, or anywhere I might find it later."

Joe busted out laughing, so did the others. He clapped me on the shoulder. "Dude, the only splooging would be in a chick's mouth." He laughed and walked out of the room.

I shook my head. "I see my work here is done." The others started to follow Joe out of the room. "I'll be back in a while; going for a ride. Chuck will be here soon."

"Cool," Joe called back.

I smirked and went to find Penelope. Leaning against the door to her room, she turned to face me, having just changed clothes.

"Too bad I didn't come any earlier. I'd have paid to see you naked again."

"Again?" she asked. "Sweetie, you only saw my back the first time. You've yet to see me naked."

There was a teasing to her voice. It was nice. "I like your choice of words. 'Yet'. Nicely done," I grinned and walked into her room. "You ready?"

"I think so. Do I need a jacket?"

"Wouldn't hurt to put one on. Mine is downstairs. Let's go."

7

The way her arms felt around my waist was like home. She belonged with me; it was only a matter of time to convince Penelope of that. I felt something with her, something I had not felt since Lexi and I were kids. I also realized I hardly knew anything about this woman, other than she loved her bass, and she just broke things off with her boyfriend. I felt, almost, like it was my lucky day… almost.

I put the kickstand down and turned off my bike. I took Penelope's hand and assisted her off of it. She removed her helmet and shook out her hair. I couldn't help but stare at this beautiful creature. The way the light shone against her face, and how her eyes lit up. She exuded beauty. Penelope did a double take and caught my gaze. She grinned and a light blush touched her cheeks.

"What is it?" she asked softly.

I shook my head. I took her helmet and sat it next to mine on the back of the bike. "You have no idea how beautiful you are." She blushed an even darker red. She turned and walked toward the edge of one of the cliffs.

"Where are we exactly?"

"Devil's Thumb area."

"Devil's Thumb?" she asked and turned back to me. I watched her for a moment and calculated the risk I was about to take. I figured she'll welcome the advance... or she'll slap me. I prayed to myself it wasn't the latter.

I nodded and stepped up behind her. My chest lightly touched against her back and I set my hands on her hips. I leaned in and spoke in a lowered tone. "Do you see what looks like a huge mound sticking up like a thumb?" I removed my hand and pointed out next to us. She followed where I motioned then she nodded. "They call it Devil's thumb because it... well, looks like a thumb."

"Why Devil's thumb?" She casually turned her head to the side and our lips were close. So close, I could smell the cherry lip-gloss. I wanted to devour her. I sighed and shrugged slightly.

"Honestly? I don't really know." Penelope grinned and shook her head. She looked back toward the raised rock with curiosity. I wanted to slip my arms around her waist and hold her close, but at the same time, I didn't want to push her. Instead, I inhaled deeply then took a step back, putting space between us.

She sighed visibly and shoved her hands in her pockets. A silence followed and it did not feel uncomfortable. I watched her hair as the wind blew it gently. She shifted her weight slightly then turned around to face me. Penelope pulled her hair behind her ears and watched the ground.

"I didn't have the best childhood." She kept her gaze down as she began to open up to me. "My mom died when I was younger. She was in a car accident."

"I'm so sorry," I told her. She looked up and grinned slightly. I had no idea what to say to this other than sorry. I had both of my parents. Not that they got along all the time, but they were still around. Hearing this, there's a good chance that I have taken that fact for granted.

"Thank you, I appreciate that." She kicked at the ground then continued. "Someone ran her off the road. It was early in the morning. Whoever did it was never found."

"Penelope," I said her name softly. She shook her head and continued.

"No, it's okay. I don't get to talk about this too often. It's sort of refreshing." She looked up at me and sighed. "My dad remarried when I got a little older. My step-monster couldn't stand the sight of me. She would frequently tell me that I was the devil's spawn and should have never been born. She also tried to blame me in my mother's death."

"Holy shit!" The words were out there before I had to think about it.

"Yeah," she mumbled and lowered her gaze. "My dad didn't stand up for me much."

"What? Why?" How could a parent not protect their children? "I'll admit, I'm not as close to my family as I probably should be... or could be, but no one has ever said anything like that to me before."

"Most parents, from what I've learned," she looked back up at me, "do not speak to their children this way." She shrugged. "First chance I had to get out, I took it. I've never gone back and seldom talk to my dad."

I had no idea what to say. I stood there and stared at this woman before me. How does one get over the torment of losing both parents? Her mother may be dead physically but her father is dead to her emotionally. I closed the distance between us and wrapped my arms around her. I pulled her against me and whispered in her hair. "Penelope, I'm so sorry. No one deserves that. I wish I could take away your pain."

She was a bit hesitant at first, but she wrapped her arms around my waist. Her cheek rested against my chest and I felt her shake slightly in my embrace. It was not my goal to make her cry... again... but no one deserves that. No one.

"Your boyfriend, how long had you two been seeing each other?"

"About two years," she hiccupped. "He was my escape. When I had enough money set aside to get my own place, he wanted to move in." Penelope pulled away and wiped at her eyes. "I told him no. I needed my own space. I needed to escape from the Hell I was in. I couldn't have him there, at least not yet. It wouldn't have been fair to him."

I thought about her words for a moment. She spoke the truth. I couldn't imagine what my band thought of my drug activity, how it had affected Lexi, and most of all, my family.

"Well," she started and took a deep breath, "it wasn't until I actually did move out that I realized my step-monster was just jealous of me."

"What? Seriously?" Penelope nodded at my words. "What in the hell was she jealous about?"

"I'm the only woman in my father's life that is permanent. That, and I am a constant reminder of my mother. I look just like her."

"Wow, that's fucked up."

She nodded. "I know. Well, I mean, I know that now. When I first left I didn't. My best friend told me I should go talk with someone. I told her I didn't need help. She said, and I quote, *everyone should seek help to get over their childhood. Everyone should go to counseling. If you haven't, you need to go.*"

"I think she's correct in her statement. I've been clean for a few years but I still talk to my counselor." I lowered my gaze. "Like, the other night at the club, I'm ashamed of what happened, but addiction is a disease." I looked up at her again and found her watching me with what looked like sadness in her eyes. "No matter what form it comes in, drugs, sex, alcohol… it's there around me all the time. It's up to me to accept that and tell it to fuck off."

"Do you mind me asking how long it took you to tell it to fuck

71

off?" She smiled softly. "I would love to tell the voices in my head that tell me I'm never good enough to fuck off."

"Whoa, are you kidding me?" I blinked watching her. She turned away from me and shook her head. "You? Not good enough? You can't honestly believe that."

She shrugged and crossed her arms over her chest. "I don't know, Blaine. I have no one. My father has disowned me and my mother is dead. I have no siblings." She sighed and was quiet for a moment. "I just have my band."

I took a few steps forward and watched her for a moment. My heart bled for her. She wanted so desperately to have what I shit on for years at a time. She just wanted someone to love her for who she was. I had that and I took advantage of it. I felt two inches tall in her presence.

Touching her shoulder, I gently turned Penelope around to face me. Her eyes downcast, I took her hands in mine and gave them a gentle squeeze. "They're your past, Penelope. Don't let them take any more of you away. You have such greatness inside of you, Hell, I feel alive when you just walk into the room."

She lifted her gaze to mine and her eyes were slightly red from crying. They shined with a fresh set of tears and she smiled. "You mean that?"

I nodded. "Of course I do. Do you have any idea... at all... how crazy I am about you?"

She laughed and shook her head. She pulled her hands from mine and turned her back to me. "Blaine..."

"I know, it's okay. I'm not asking for anything, I just need you to know that you're amazing. Fuck them."

Glancing over her shoulder at me, she grinned. "Fuck them?"

"Fuck. Them."

She nodded and turned back to the view of the mountain side. The hills were beautiful with trees of green. Roofs of homes lined the city of Boulder. Penelope sighed and I watched her while she lowered her head.

"I don't know why I allow them to continue to take from me." Her voice was almost a whisper. If I had not been paying attention, I might have missed it.

"Because you're human," I told her. "If you didn't feel this way, there would be something seriously wrong with you."

My voice was sarcastic and she picked up on it. She laughed then looked over at me. "You seem to take things so... I don't know. Laid back?"

I shrugged. "I guess that's something I have had to learn. When I got clean, I saw the world a little differently. I saw how my actions hurt those around me. I knew if I was to really make a go at being clean, I knew I needed to make up for my mistakes." I gave her a one sided grin. "It all started when I apologized, first to my family, then to my band. Thankfully, they all forgave me. I could have lost everything when I overdosed; that's what changed it all."

"Do you mind me asking what happened?"

I shook my head. "Not at all." I explained to her how I was found on the side of the road the night I snorted all my coke and swallowed all the ecstasy I had. Going through the story has made me feel a little numb. "My mother stayed with me the entire time I was in the hospital. Chuck was there most days as well."

"Chuck seems to really care about you," she offered.

I nodded. "He does, in his own way. He looks out for us and kept most of what happened out of the press. Trust me; I seriously fucked up. Now, I make up for what I did by volunteering at the Narcotics Anonymous meetings for teens. It was court ordered at first, but once my probation was over, I wanted to continue. I don't want to be the reason someone falls. I want to be the reason they said no."

"Wow, Blaine, that's amazing. There needs to be more people like you in the world."

I chuckled and shook my head. "Nah, one of me is enough." She smiled. "It took me hitting rock bottom to realize this, Penelope. I wouldn't wish my detox on my worst enemy." I lowered my gaze and sighed. Recalling how it made me feel, how worthless, out of control, and how I wanted to die most days. Detox for me was the hardest time I can ever remember.

"You have an amazing story, Blaine." She stepped closer and gently touched my bicep.

I looked into her eyes and smiled. "So do you."

$\sim$

A few hours passed and we'd decided it was time to head back. The sharing of our lives became pretty heavy and we both felt it was time to relax. A party would be happening at the house tonight. Penelope had not met the entire band yet and I knew she was excited.

I turned on the bike and it roared to life. She slipped her helmet on and slid her arms around my waist. She leaned into my body and I knew our time together had allowed us to bond as friends. She knew now that she could trust me, which is what I'd wanted. That trust is something I would never take for granted. I wanted Penelope... needed Penelope to be mine. If love was an addiction, she was definitely my drug of choice. I felt myself falling for this woman. I adored everything about her; the way she held herself under pressure, the way she allowed crap to roll off her shoulders, even the way she spoke of her parents. Most people I know can't handle the shit she has been through. Hell, a part of me wondered how she's been handling it all these years. I don't imagine her recent ex had a huge role in it. I also wondered if he knew half of what she told me.

We pulled into my garage and we dismounted. The music inside was thumping and I grinned. "Well, sounds like the party has indeed started." I held my elbow out for her. "Shall we?"

She slipped her hand around my arm and returned my smile. "Ooh, let's!"

We walked inside and Penelope gasped aloud. My band was here and damn did they sound good.

I led Penelope toward the jam room. I had this room set up a few years ago for us to practice in. Inside, the music travels. The outside of the house was sound proofed. Chuck loved this and we did many practices here.

Deep Ember was set up in the room and they were playing one of our latest hits. I glanced over at Penelope and she had a look of being awestruck. I chuckled and pulled her closer to me.

"Go in and introduce yourself. They already know who you are." Watching her was like Christmas morning; the excitement at finding what I'd been asking for the most inside a wrapped gift. She was the beautiful wrapped gift to me. She grinned at me and her eyes lit up like a beautiful pair of sapphires.

8

*M*att was hitting the skins and his head banged with the music. He grinned across the room when he saw me standing in the doorway with Penelope. She stepped closer and the grin on her face showed her excitement.

There she goes, just a walking down the street singin'...
Doo wa ditty ditty dum ditty do!

Penelope's eyes widened and the band laughed. Derek started the chorus and without missing a beat, the others chimed in. This wasn't our style music but it was fun nonetheless.

"About time you two came back," Derek offered. "You ready to sing?" He asked, looking at me.

"Hell yeah!" I closed the distance to the mic and took it in my hand. "You sounded great, man." I clapped Derek on his back and turned to face our audience... Mongrels of Soul. I glanced over at Matt, *"Lizards or lime?"* He nodded and counted off the beat.

The music poured through the speakers and my voice sang through the mic. *Lizards or lime* was our first charting single and we were damn proud of it. Writing the lyrics with Matt, we'd had this song recorded, and on the radio faster than anyone thought possible. Later, when it released with the album, it grossed double what we'd anticipated. Deep Ember would be big. I'd known it. Chuck had known it. My drug habit had also known it.

The evening we found out our album went platinum, I snorted a lot of coke and pot was smoked like cigarettes. It wasn't one of my finer moments. Looking back on things now, I am grateful for the overdose. The thought is odd to consider, but without that moment in my life, I wouldn't be clean now, wouldn't have met Mongrels of Soul, and ultimately, would not have met Penelope.

I glanced at her as I sang and her eyes never left mine. It felt like she could see into my soul. It honestly scared the hell out of me, but in the same breath, it was exciting. It was also relieving. This woman knew what I had been through and didn't judge me for it. She was an angel… she was my goddess. If only she felt the same about me.

In that moment, I broke the gaze we had with one another. It hurt me to have my heart on my sleeve and for her not to accept it. I knew she was hurting from her break up, but I think she'd known it was over a long time ago. Sometimes, admitting defeat is as tough as living in denial.

"The Nile is a river, not a condition." The therapist at the NA center told me this one day and the words have never left my mind. At first, I was confused by the meaning then later realized the Nile represented "nial", as in denial. Clever.

The song ended and I put the mic back into the stand. I turned to the band and raised my arms in the air. "Tonight is about music, friends, and sex. You play it, listen to it, or fuck it!"

The guys all cheered. I chuckled and, when I turned back to Penelope, she was blushing. I grinned and started to walk out of the room. "Grabbing a drink; who wants something?"

"Me!" Matt shouted. "Get me a beer!"

"Get it yourself," called Chuck as he walked into the room. "I have some news, guys. Take a moment and set your equipment down."

I paused by the entryway and leaned against the wall. I looked over at Penelope as she took a seat on the floor. She glanced in my direction with a concerned look. I shrugged my shoulders and mouthed, *I don't know.*

"I was able to book Deep Ember for a private show in two days. It's a moneymaking opportunity and Mongrels of Soul; you'll be in the VIP booth and green room. When the tickets were listed, they sold out in about fifteen minutes."

"Whoa, damn!" Matt called. "We've never sold out that fast!"

"You're playing in your home state, kids. Get ready to rock the fucking House of Blues." Chuck held up his beer and saluted the crowd. "You deserve a party. Now," he turned back to face me, "you can go get his beer, bitch." Chuck laughed at his own joke.

My eyes widened a bit in shock. I knew he was teasing but calling me a bitch? Well, that was a little too far. Time to play with fire. "That's not what your girl said last night." I smirked and started to back out of the door.

"What the fuck did you say?" He yelled as his face started turning red.

"She begged to call me daddy!" I laughed as I took off running. Chuck could kick my ass and I knew it. But I also enjoyed teasing the fucker; it was too easy. Hell, he made it too easy.

"Chuck," Penelope offered. Her voice was loud enough to catch his attention. I felt myself strain to hear her voice. "He was with me last night. Don't worry; he definitely wasn't with your girl."

"What?" Chuck and Derek both asked at the same time. I'm glad I was listening now. This was about to get real interesting.

"He felt sick and asked me to hold back his hair back while he worshiped the porcelain god," she offered.

It was quiet for a moment that is until I heard a snort in the room. The snort came from Matt. They all knew I had not been sick.

"I pulled his head back and yelled at him, who's your daddy now, bitch?" Penelope grinned and got to her feet.

"Dude," Matt started, "you seriously allowed chick to treat you like you were HER bitch?" He laughed behind the drums and the others soon followed suite.

"Yeah," I glared at Penelope with a smirk, "sure did. Tonight though, tonight she'll beg to call me daddy."

Penelope's mouth dropped open, and she shook her head. "Whatever! Now, can we please get over ourselves and play some fucking music?"

I chuckled under my breath and stood leaning against the wall. She was definitely playful when her guard was down. A shadow draped the floor, followed by Chuck. I glanced up to him and grinned.

"You're an asshole," he told me then he grinned. "I don't know what you did but the chick in there obviously cares about you."

"What's that supposed to mean? What I did? She's a kind person. Do I not deserve someone to be considerate toward me?"

"Not when she's taking care of you. She barely knows you, kid." He dug his index finger into my chest. "Be careful with her."

"You'd be surprised how much we know about each other and don't touch me like that. You turn me on." I winked at him and Chuck rolled his eyes. He knows I'm joking around, always the kidder.

"I'm glad to see you've been sober this long. You've done great, kid. Keep it up." He gripped my shoulder then turned to leave.

"Will you give me a golden star for good behavior?" I grinned and made my way toward the fridge for the beer.

"Yeah, I'll tattoo it on your forehead, fucker. Now get in there and sing something."

Chuck left the room and headed down toward the recording area. He'd either be making calls for more shows or he just wanted some quiet time. Hell, if he ever wanted quiet time he was in the wrong line of business.

I grabbed a few beers and the cold glass felt foreign in my hands. As much as I wanted a drink, I had a feeling it would taste sour in my mouth. I took them into the room and sat them on a wooden table in the corner by a bay window. As I was turning to leave, I glanced over at Penelope and found her watching me. She smiled and slowly looked away. Oh... what a tease this girl was.

I started making my way toward her when the doorbell rang. A few minutes later, some people we knew... some of them we trusted... showed up. Some were groupies, others were hard core fans. Our fan base started with our closest friends then, slowly, began extending outward. It was easy to know who was here for us and who was here to benefit themselves. The latter were never invited to parties like this.

Soon, booze would be entertaining our party guests here. The rule was no drugs, but it was never guaranteed. The women dressed like they had razors in their clothes. Everything had a tear and their breasts were pouring out of their shirts. As much as I would love to sink into one of them, the only one I wanted right now was Penelope.

They knew their part and never forgot their place. They had their own little group in a way. They knew us as individuals and as a band. They had probably slept with each of us, but never let it get weird. Every once in a while, they felt like one of the guys... but with tits.

"Blaine! Hey baby, where've you been?" one of the girls, Monique, asked. Her hair was dyed almost a white blonde, her brown eyes were lined with eye liner so heavy you could barely see her eyes. Her clothes were at least one size too small and her frame was tiny. She was a sight to see, but not for me, not tonight.

Monique made her way across the room and hugged me. She purposely pressed her body against mine so I would notice her tits. Hell, they were hard not to notice.

"Hey girl," I said and hugged her back. "Good to see ya." She leaned in to kiss me and I quickly averted it. "Whoa girl, not tonight." I backed away and she gave me pouty lips.

"Aww, why not?" she pouted again and stuck out her painted red lips. She'd had her lips around my cock once. Damn she was good at it, too. I glanced across the room and found Derek watching her. I pulled her close and she suddenly got excited.

"I tell you what; I'm not available tonight," she whined and pouted again, "but, I know someone who is." I pointed over at Derek and his eyes suddenly widened. "That there is the lead singer for Mongrels of Soul. I'm producing their band. Go chat him up a while. He's into you, Monique." I watched as she smiled then gently nudged her along. Derek glanced at me, then at Monique, then back at me. He grinned and I nodded at him.

I made my way over to Penelope and raised a single brow, before I smirked.

"The skirt she's wearing could probably double as a tube top," she claimed. "She is going to seriously hurt Derek, you know that?"

I chuckled then shrugged. "She'll ride him hard and hang him up wet."

"That's so gross," Penelope said and made a face at me.

I laughed again and shook my head. "Want to sing or play?"

"I do, but before I pick up anything, was all that… was it for me?" Her eyes looked up into mine and the vulnerability shot me straight through the heart. Damn, this girl had me and she had no idea how bad.

"If it was, does it matter?" I asked.

She nodded. "It does."

"Okay, then yes, it was for you."

She smiled then walked past me, her shoulder barely brushing against mine. I watched her as she stopped and stood in place for a moment. I figured she was thinking what she would play when she suddenly turned on me. Penelope quickly kissed me on my lips and held it for a few seconds.

I didn't breathe, I didn't move and I definitely didn't push her away. When she finally pulled back, she smiled, and looked into my eyes. "Keep it up. There might be more later."

I've never had a goofy moment around a woman who has

swept me off my feet, but I'm sure I just had one. I smiled and I'm damn positive it was a goofy grin because all I heard after that was laughter from both bands.

~

a few hours had passed and it was well into the night. Booze was flowing and people would leave the room from time to time, most likely getting high outside. I kept my bottle of water in hand and had busied myself between playing and entertaining Penelope. They all knew I didn't want the shit around, but I also wasn't stupid. Music and drugs was something that existed together in most situations. It was up to each of us to make the call if we wanted involvement or not. It was too easy to score and even easier at parties. It was definitely hard to watch, but being sober and in a safe environment, like my home, I knew I could retreat and find sanctuary in my own space if I needed.

Penelope had a set of lungs on her and she sang into the mic as if she were making love to it. The woman could hypnotize a crowd in mere seconds. She took control and maintained it with ease. This was something to be had; the woman appeared to be submissive but now, while holding the power in her hands, she was a Domme. Damn, she was hot and it made my dick spring to life.

She would occasionally look at me as she sang her lyrics, she would wet her lips with her tongue, and her body would sway with the rhythm of the song. Her knees would bend and she would arch her back while singing her music. The woman was a goddess.

The tempo changed and, immediately, I recognized the song they were about to play. Joan Jett's *I Love Rock & Roll* started up and Penelope squealed with excitement.

I saw him dancing there by the record machine

I knew he must have been about seventeen
The beat was going strong
Playing my favorite song
And I could tell it wouldn't be long till he was with me
Yeah me
And I could tell it wouldn't be long till he was with me
Yeah me
Singing, I love rock and roll
So put another dime in the jukebox, baby...

When she sang *"rock and roll"* each of us raised our voices and sang as loud as we could. As she repeated the chorus, she held the mic out and everyone sang for her. She was alive and she was here, ready to rock everyone to their core. I knew I was right in putting her up front. The woman could captivate an audience. She was the magic that turned heads.

I glanced over at Derek and not a jealous feature played on the man's face. That was a very good thing. The last thing I needed was a jealous front man.

Acknowledge the gifts of those around you and build on it. Become stronger. Be THE band, not just A band.

Chuck's words rang through my mind for a moment. He was a genius with us and here he was, doing it again. The man had a gift.

When the song ended, Penelope put the mic up and waved at Derek to come take her place. He sprinted toward the open area and pulled her into a hug. He said something to her and she squealed. I couldn't hear them over the crowd cheering her on, but I could assume it was good.

I smiled at her when she looked my way. She came running off the stage area and immediately hugged me. "That was so amazing! Holy shit!"

"You looked amazing up there," I told her. She laughed and bounced in place with excitement.

"I need a drink!"

"What's your poison?" I asked her. I waved down one of my staff in the room who came over in a few, short strides.

"Vodka tonic," she told him. He nodded and left us.

"Feel like dancing?" I asked her then waggled my brows.

She giggled. "You bet! But I warn you, I'm a professional out there." She held her hands above her head like a ballerina then did a spin.

"Clearly," I said with a grin. Penelope turned away from me smiling. She was full of happiness and possibly gratitude. I suppose time would tell if it was gratitude for the situation or to her saving. All I knew was, after saving myself, she'd stepped in and given me a reason to want to be here... even in an atmosphere containing drugs.

I followed closely behind as we headed toward the makeshift dance floor. She moved to the rhythm of the music in a sultry way. Her hips swayed and, as she turned to face me, her arms went over her head. She ran her fingers through her hair, tilted her head back, and pushed out her breasts. Penelope grinded her hips against an invisible force and the force was my cock. Good lord, could she move.

My fist found its way into my mouth and I bit down on it. I couldn't move; I could only stare. I wanted her in the worst way. I wanted... no needed her to be mine and know how much she meant to me. My need was not purely animalistic, but it was damn close. I wouldn't lie to myself and say the attraction is what was driving this. It's not, but it definitely aids to the effect of it.

She opened her eyes and watched me... watching her. "Dance with me." She reached for my hands and pulled me closer. I stared down into her eyes and was mesmerized. She smiled and let go of my hands just to put hers around my neck. "What's the matter? Kitty got your tongue?" She grinned and she knew, without a shadow of a doubt, how I felt.

"No, not quite a kitty, but definitely a Penny." I winked and she grinned. She removed her hands from my neck and placed them on my chest. Penelope moved her hips in a way that should be illegal. She was dancing against me as if she was a stripper and I was her pole. Fuck, I wanted to be her pole.

She lowered herself, and her head was level with my cock… and she knew it. If there was ever a time my cock could spring from my pants, it would do it right now. She had me hard without even touching me.

Penelope gripped my hips and rose; her breasts brushed against me. I groaned out loud and I know she heard me. I watched her face blush slightly.

"I'm sorry," she said in a lowered voice.

"Are you kidding?" I asked with a single raised brow. "Fuck, I'm not. Do it again."

She laughed and shook her head. Penelope turned and, with her back to me, began to dance. Her ass rubbed against my crotch and it took everything I had to not bend her over and take her right then; to hell with those in the room watching.

Looking back over her shoulder, she winked. Fuck me; I'm dead. Whether she realized it yet or not, Penelope and I are going to become very familiar with one another tonight. I grabbed her hips and brought her hard against me. Her eyes widened a little then a smirk took her lips.

Standing straight again, she danced, and raised her arms. She wrapped one around my neck and pulled me close, my chest firm against her back. My hands moved around her hips and maneuvered over her stomach. Damn, was it flat and strong. I imagined, for a moment, what it would be like to lick her from her tits to her folds.

She pulled me closer to her as she tilted her head toward me. I cupped her cheek with my hand and closed the gap between us as my lips claimed hers. Her lips were like warm, soft cherry pie and her tongue glided with mine. I could barely taste the Vodka on her tongue. I'm not sure when we stopped dancing, but at some point, we stopped moving.

"Get a room!" Unfortunately, our moment ended when someone yelled out in the mic. She pulled away and when she opened her eyes, we held each other's gaze for a moment then she looked away with a smile.

I glanced up to the mic and found Joe. I frowned, then yelled, "Shouldn't you be on the drums, dip shit?" He laughed and flipped me off. I chuckled and looked back at Penelope. "You want to get out of here?" She nodded then took my hand. She led me toward the bar and asked for a double vodka over ice. They handed it over and she took a long pull.

I took her hand and lead her out of the room and through the kitchen. She pulled me to a stop once the music became nothing but a dull thump. She swayed slightly where she stood. "Blaine?"

I smiled and touched her cheek. She looked beautiful, standing here in my den. I wanted to ravage her. I wanted to lick her body. More than anything, I wanted to make love to her. "Yes?"

Taking in a deep breath, she looked down. "I... You scare me."

"What?" This was not what I had expected. "I scare you?"

She nodded. "Yeah," she glanced back up, "you're amazing. You've been so good to me and listened when I needed you to. You didn't rush me and even after knowing your reputation, you just seem so... different." Ahh, there it is. The truth is out. She's scared of my past. Hell, I am, too. "I need a drink," she groaned and finished off her double shot of Vodka.

"Penelope, trust me when I tell you, I am not my past." I cupped her cheeks and stepped closer. "I'm a better man than I was ever before. I've been sober for a couple of years and honestly, since I've met you, you've given me a new reason to be clean."

"I have?" She smiled as she stared at me. Her eyes began to glaze slightly.

I nodded. "Absolutely. I've wanted you for a long time. I'm sure you know that." She blushed and lowered her eyes. "No, baby, look at me."

"Baby?" she asked and lifted her gaze.

"Yeah, baby. Now I want you to hear me when I say this. I want you. No one else; just you. You're different; you're not like the others. I find myself thinking about you all the time. What you want when you get up. What you think about when you're alone. What you dream about. What I'm trying to say is…" I paused and took a deep breath, then slowly exhaled, "baby I've fallen hard for you. I'm done. I want… no, I need, you to be mine."

Her eyes began to shine. A tear slipped down her cheek in a fast streak. She smiled and her bottom lip trembled slightly. "Oh Blaine…" She leaned in closer and gripped my arms.

We stood there for what felt like hours… but it was mere seconds. I could hear my pulse pounding in my head as I waited for her answer. I felt my heart race and perspiration build on my brow. "Penelope, please," I begged of her, "I want to be yours."

"I want to be yours, Blaine." she smiled and continued, "I also want you to be mine."

I sighed. "Why do I feel like there's about to be a but."

She laughed. "You have a nice butt."

I shook my head. "Thank you, although that's not what I meant." I winked.

"There is a but; but it's not what you think."

"Okay," I paused and waited for her. I felt like I would jump out of my skin if she didn't get to her point. I needed this woman and I felt like I was on a cliff, teetering between salvation and falling to my death.

"But… I just need you to be patient with me." She swayed slightly and continued. "I have a lot of shit in my past and I need to know you'll be there to help me get through it. I know it's a lot to ask, but there it is."

"That's it?" I asked her. She looked a little taken aback, but slowly, she nodded.

"Gravy. What else?"

Her brows rose in surprise. "Really? No questions or concerns?"

"Nope. You told me about your family and I know about your ex. You know my past and how I shit on those around me." I shrugged and grinned at her. "We know each other's shit and yet, here we are."

"Here we are," she repeated with a smile. She tilted her head slightly. "Then kiss me, dammit."

"Oh, hell yeah!" I pulled her flush against me and kissed her with everything I had. She whimpered softly and her body melted into mine. Her lips were soft and warm. They were welcoming and submissive as I tilted her head back slightly. I could taste the Vodka on her mouth and it pulled me in closer. I moved my hands down her waist, to her ass. I gripped it for a moment and appreciated how she filled my palms. I loved a nice ass on a woman and Penelope definitely packed a nice one.

She wrapped her arms tight around my neck. I lifted her and she wrapped her slender legs around my waist. I carried her to my room and kicked the door open, then pushed it closed with my back.

I had not expected this moment to occur, but I damn sure hoped it would. Her fingers moved into my hair and she tugged it, pulling my head back. She deepened our kiss and moaned into my mouth.

I turned us and pressed her against the wall. My hands moved up her body and I appreciated the curves of her waist. I wanted more; I needed more. I needed her and needed to be inside her. "I need you," I whispered against her lips.

"Then take me," she answered and gently nibbled my lip.

My dick responded with a throb. She began to grind her hips against me. I groaned and gripped her hips tighter. "Fuck woman!"

"Exactly," she mumbled with a soft moan.

That's all I needed. I carried her to the bed and laid us down.

Her legs remained wrapped around my waist and I moved on top of her. We kissed harder and leaning to the side, I grasped her breast with my hand. She filled it completely and she arched into my touch. Her bra was thin and I felt her nipple harden against my palm. Fuck... I wanted to suck on her tit.

"Get me out of my clothes," she mumbled against my lips. I pulled back and looked down into her eyes. My fingers gently touched her cheek and she smiled. "What is it?" her voice sounded slightly concerned.

I shook my head. "You're beautiful and I'm a lucky son of a bitch." She smiled and pressed her hands against my chest. We sat up and Penelope tugged at the hem of my shirt. She pulled it over my head and tossed it. She leaned and kissed across my chest.

My head tilted back and my lips parted. I sighed, enjoying this moment with this woman... my woman. Lowering my head, I grabbed a fistful of hair and pulled her head back. She gasped and I claimed her lips, while my other hand kneaded her breast. Her fingers fumbled with my pants and I pulled from her lips.

"I'll take care of these. Let's get you out of yours." Penelope lifted her arms above her head. I grabbed her shirt and pulled it off her. Her breasts were covered in a sheer, black bra. I could see her nipples through it and one of them was pierced. I grinned. "Well, what do we have here? Damn baby, this is fucking hot." I glanced at her and she smiled then looked back down.

Penelope hiccupped then giggled at herself. I was beginning to lean in to capture her nipple in my mouth when I looked up. She grinned and swayed slightly.

I sighed and my head dropped between my shoulders. "Fucking perfect," I mumbled to myself.

"Blaine, baby, what is it?" She ran her fingers through my hair and more than anything, I wanted to have sex with this woman. I also wanted her sober when it happened.

Lifting my head, I looked into her eyes. "Nothing, baby. Relax and lay down. I'll take care of you real soon."

"Oh, goodie!" she giggled and lay back on my bed.

I finally get the perfect woman to admit her feelings for me and she's drunk. I sighed and rose from the bed. I removed her boots then slid her skirt down. "Damn, your panties had to match your bra?" I could see right through them. She had waxed recently and I wanted so desperately to taste her.

Instead, I groaned... loud... and tugged my comforter up around her. She pulled her arms out and relaxed into the bed. Within a few minutes, Penelope had passed out. I sat down on the side of the bed and watched her for a moment. I smiled at her and touched her cheek.

Countless times I had sex while drunk and high... sometimes just high. Some of the women I didn't remember. Many of them were just as drunk or high.

I rose from the bed and made my way to the bathroom. I turned on the shower and removed my clothes. My dick was fucking hard and I didn't want blue balls. I could jerk it off in the shower but it wouldn't be Penelope. Sighing long... with a groan... I stepped inside and allowed the cold water to hit my skin. I wanted to yell but didn't. I wanted to jump out but didn't. I wanted to sober Penelope up then make love to her... but didn't.

My forearm rested against the tile wall and I laid my head on it. "Fuck my life," I groaned.

After a few minutes of torture by ice-cold water, I stepped out and dried off. I hung my towel then looked into my bedroom. Penelope was still asleep. I sighed and walked in naked. I pulled on a pair of boxer briefs from inside my dresser. As I looked upon her still form, my heart felt as if it would leap from my chest. I hated this, hated not having control over my feelings.

Keeping people at bay, keeping them at arm's length worked for me. Never letting the guard down insured I would never be the one to get hurt. Now, all bets were off. My heart was on the table and Penelope had the ability to hold it in her hands.

Would she squeeze it? Would she hold it for her own? I

honestly had no idea. I stepped up to the bed and slid inside, next to her. She turned on her side and her arm wrapped around my chest.

"Hold me," she mumbled. I slid an arm under her pillow then nudged her toward me. I pulled her close and she laid her head in the crook of my shoulder. She snuggled in even closer. The way her body felt against mine was like being at home. She was warm, she smelled like her shampoo and body soap. I could faintly smell the telltale scent of alcohol.

I watched her until her breathing grew deeper and I knew she had fallen into a deep sleep. Slowly, my eyes began to drift closed as I lay next to the woman that had stolen my heart, the woman I had fallen hard for.

9

The next morning, the sun shone in through my bedroom window. The warmth of it beamed across my face. I squinted faintly then turned away from it. My arms tightened around Penelope's sleeping form. I kissed the side of her shoulder lightly and mumbled, "Good morning."

"Mmm..." She stretched lightly in my arms then groaned. "Oh, I need a pain killer for this hangover. Why did you let me drink so much?"

"As if it were my fault," I chuckled into her neck.

Suddenly, her body became stiff next to mine. She slowly turned her head to face me and her eyes immediately went wide. "Oh, SHIT!" Penelope quickly scrambled to sit up and pulled the sheets to her neck. She pulled them back just enough to look down then pulled them close again. She looked at me, then the door, then back at me. Her breathing turned into what sounded like panic. "How? What? Who..."

"Calm down," I told her. I pulled my arms behind my head and grinned. I figured she's in freak out mode, thinking that I had taken advantage and fucked her. Well, since she seems to think so highly of me, I decided I'd have a little fun... at her expense, since

I'm such an upstanding guy in her book. To be honest, it hurt... a lot.

"Don't you remember anything from last night?" I winked at her and she gasped.

"Oh shit... Oh SHIT!" She cupped her face and sat there for a moment. I wanted to chuckle, I wanted to tell her nothing happened but I figured, why not allow her imagination to fill her in. I'm curious what she thought had happened.

"You weren't saying that last night, baby."

She peeked at me through the sheets then shook her head. "What... oh shit Blaine, what happened last night?"

"You're kidding, right?" I sat up and allowed the sheets to fall away from me. All she could see was my bare chest and arms. My boxer briefs were still slightly covered.

Her eyes trailed over my body and the look of confusion turned to fear. "Oh shit, we slept together?" Penelope's face dropped in color and her back hit the headboard of my bed. "How do I not remember this?"

I feigned shock. "You don't remember yelling my name, followed by harder, faster and oh my god, don't stop? Hell, woman, you begged me to slap your ass."

Her eyes shifted to mine and she studied me for a moment. I couldn't hold it in any longer. I began to crack a slight smile and snorted. The chuckle turned into an outright laugh. "Penelope, you seriously think I would take advantage of you like that?" I shook my head. "I'm only teasing here, but honestly, I'm a little hurt." I threw the covers back and stood. Morning wood wasn't forgiving and I knew she saw my cock stretched through my underwear... well if her widened eyes were any indication...

"Nothing happened between us, I promise. We came up here and I thought it would have, but you passed out on me. I would never take advantage of you that way." I considered my words while I watched her expression shift from fear to remorse. "Oh yeah, you have a lot of making up to do." I grinned and turned my back to her as I made my way to the bathroom.

If I was being honest with myself, it hurt a lot more than I'd let on that she could even consider the possibility of me hurting her. I enjoyed having her in my arms and in my bed. I would be lying if I said it didn't turn me on. Her body was slender and tight. Her hair draped down her body and tickled my skin. Her skin was soft and it begged to be gripped. Her tits were round and damn, I wanted to suck them. I wanted to peel her panties down and sink my mouth into her, taste her pussy. I wanted to do so many things to this woman and fuck; my dick throbbed for a needed release.

I gripped my boxers and quickly pulled them down. My balls were sore and, as I stood, Penelope suddenly made a noise somewhere between a scream and a squeal.

She covered her face and stood there in my bathroom door. I have no idea how long she'd been standing there, but it was at least long enough to get a full view of me naked. I chuckled.

"Well, now that you've seen me, care to shower and wash my back?"

"Oh my god!" She continued to stand there, probably in shock.

"If you turn the other way, you can uncover your eyes and walk out, that is if that's what you want to do."

Her voice was muffled under her hands. "Oh Blaine, I'm so embarrassed!" She peeked through her fingers and gasped, then turned her back to me. I chuckled again.

"Seriously, Penelope, I wonder if you have ever seen a cock before in your life." I couldn't help the grin on my face.

"I've seen cock before, thank you! Just... never yours."

Even with her back to me, I could see her neck and ears had turned red. I grinned even wider. "No, you can't say that now. You've seen it." I pursed my lips and stepped closer. I tried not to touch her with my length as I leaned into her ear and whispered. "Want to touch it?"

She jumped forward, startled, and quickly turned back. Her

face was uncovered and she looked down, then back up. She lifted a hand to shield her face and I could see a smile on her lips.

"Ahhh, caught you looking!"

"You're incorrigible!" she huffed and stood there. I laughed again and shook my head.

"The shower option is still on the table," I winked.

She kept her hand up to block the view of my cock and stared at me. "No. I'll see you downstairs. Clothed!" Penelope took another glance down through her fingers then looked to me. "Nice package, by the way," she blushed again then finally left the bathroom.

I chuckled and turned to face my shower. I have no idea why she came to the bathroom, unless it had been to tell me something. Guess I'll have to get that from her later. Until then, I now had this amazing, fantastic memory of her to keep in my bank. If this woman does end up with me, which is now my plan, I plan to remind her of this moment… daily.

I heard my bedroom door shut and I had to smile when I considered her walk of shame. If anyone were to see her leave my bedroom, they would automatically assume she'd slept with me. It wouldn't be that far from the truth. She had slept next to me.

The hot water hit my body as I stepped inside the shower. Considering the hard on I had, the water should have been set to cold. At the moment, I didn't care. Leaning against the wall, my hand wrapped around my cock and I stroked it. I closed my eyes and thought of Penelope; the kissing, the touching… everything we did before she'd passed out.

I imagined her lips… soft and full. The way she would look on her knees servicing me. Fuck, I needed her more than she knew. Sex appeal was definitely on the agenda, but so was the way I felt for her. I didn't just want to fuck her, I wanted to please her, show her I cared for her.

Suddenly lyrics came to mind.

Bring me back from the brink
You're my missing link
Lay down beside me
Hold me through the dark of night
Stop the fright
And heal me with your touch

I felt my cock throb and I knew I was close. I stroked faster until I finally came with a groan. Fuck, I needed this release more than I realized. "Now to go back and tell everyone I thought of lyrics while jerking off in the shower." I chuckled and shook my head.

~

I made my way downstairs to have breakfast. Penelope was sitting alone in the breakfast nook with her notepad out. I didn't want to disturb her but she apparently heard me approach. She looked over and I paused in my step. We held one another's gaze for a moment then she offered a small smile and looked away.

Rather than starting a conversation on an assumption, I decided to keep my thoughts to myself. After pouring a glass of orange juice, I took a seat across from her and looked out the window. I could feel the tension coming from her and it was hard to not say anything... or even look at her. She'd seen me naked and it bothered her. She'd also thought I'd taken advantage of her and that seriously bothered me.

"Are you going to look at me?" she finally asked.

"I don't know," I answered her. "I know you're embarrassed, but honestly, I'm hurt."

"How did I hurt you?" The sting was in her voice and she apparently has no idea how she has affected me.

I took another drink of my juice and sat my glass down. My

fingers folded on the table, I took a deep breath then slowly exhaled as I looked up. Dramatics were not exactly my strong suit, unless I was high. I clearly wasn't, so I had an idea. I wasn't sure if this would work or not. I didn't want to lose it again and laugh at the situation earlier, but at the same time, Penelope needed to understand how I felt. She needed to know how her actions had hurt me.

After I exhaled, I finally looked into her eyes. Hurt, fear, and desperation lingered behind them. I'm not sure if it's because of our awkward moment, or something else.

"When we woke up this morning, it was one of the best mornings I've had in a very, very long time."

"Blaine," she started and I held up my hand to stop her.

"Please, you asked, let me finish."

"Alright." She sat back in her seat and watched me. She raised a single brow and drummed her fingers on her arm.

I sighed and shifted in my seat. I glanced out the window and watched as a squirrel ran up a tree. "Penelope, waking up next to you was the highlight of my morning. Hell, it'll be the highlight of my damn week." Looking back at her, Penelope's features shifted from impatience to confusion. I was right in my assumption; she had no idea.

"When you woke and realized you were in my bed, you automatically thought the worst. It wasn't that you thought the situation was bad, it was the fact you even considered I would do that to you."

"Oh my... Blaine, I..." she shook her head and continued to stare at me. As much as I wanted to tease her about seeing me naked earlier, I needed her to understand how much her actions had cut me.

"I don't need you to explain anything, Penelope. I just need you to understand..." I lowered my head until my chin was just above my chest. "You cut me deeply." I pushed away from the table with intentions to leave her with her thoughts.

"Blaine, stop." Her voice was commanding. I felt myself stop and I stood there, my back to her.

"What? I mean seriously," I turned to face her. "I get it that I have a reputation and shit, but seriously, I thought you knew I respected you and would never, ever do that." I shook my head.

"Blaine, would you stop a minute? Geez, you're such a bitch sometimes!" She stood and walked around the table until she was directly in front of me.

"A bitch? I assure you, I'm not a bitch, nor will I ever be anyone's bitch."

She smirked. "So not what I meant." Penelope shifted where she stood. I could see the words churning in her head as she watched me. I raised my brows in an effort to get her to talk. She sighed then lowered her gaze. "I'm sorry," she told me. "I truly am. I didn't mean to hurt you and I know I did." She looked back up, "I guess, well there's no excuse other than reactive instinct."

"Reactive instinct? To what, exactly?" I crossed my arms over my chest and tilted my head slightly. This ought to be good. She kept my gaze for a moment and I could see her growing uncomfortable. A part of me wanted to pull her close and tell her it would be okay, that I forgave her. The other part was still pissed she thought so little of me. I wanted to punch the shit out of the other side, tell it to shut the fuck up. As much as I wanted people to forgive me for my actions, I knew, deep inside, I also needed to forgive myself.

"I don't know."

"Yes you do. Just say it."

"What do you want me to say? That I thought you used me like one of your groupies?"

I flinched slightly at her words. "Did you really think that?"

She shook her head. "No, I didn't. Just... I don't remember much of the night after my third or fourth shot. I'm not a heavy or recreational drinker." She shrugged. "I do remember us kissing though." She met my gaze again.

I raised a brow. "You… remember that?"

She nodded and smiled. "Yeah, it was… nice." She blushed, and then smiled bigger.

"Well," I took a step forward, "it was nice. You let your guard down and had a great time. I'll be honest. I really wanted to sleep with you, but the moment I realized you had too much to drink was just before you passed out. I removed your boots and tucked you in."

"That's all that happened?" She was vulnerable and it was all over her face.

I nodded. "You asked me to hold you then I copped a feel."

She gasped and shook her head in denial.

"Cool it, woman; the last part I'm teasing. Well, sort of. Before you passed out, we were kind of all over one another." I winked at her. Penelope shook her head again and grinned.

"Remind me next time we decide to make out, no alcohol."

"Oh," I stepped closer until we were barely a breath's distance apart. As we looked into one another's eyes, I swear this woman could see directly into my soul. "So you're saying there will be another make out session in the near future?" I grinned and swept my finger down her cheek.

"Only if you agree not to drop trou in the bathroom again." Her face lit up bright red and she giggled. "I can't believe I saw you naked!"

"You saw Blaine naked?" Matt's voice came into the kitchen then he started laughing. "So was his pecker like, super small? Because I heard…"

"Shut your fucking mouth!" I yelled at my best friend. He laughed and ran from the room. Penelope laughed as well then covered her lips.

"I'm sorry," she whispered through her fingers.

"Don't be. You saw it; you know I don't have a super small pecker, as Matt has been led to believe."

She laughed again. "Pecker?"

I grinned and shrugged. "His words, not mine." She laughed once again and I loved how it lit up her face. She was beautiful. I cupped her face and gently tilted her face up to mine. "Now, if you don't mind," I leaned in and gently kissed her on the lips. Penelope kissed me back and leaned into me. I wanted more than anything to deepen it, to kiss her more, but after this morning, I needed to give her time.

She was still fresh from her break up and the thought of me taking advantage of her still stung. I let her go and took a step back. The look of remorse touched her features as she watched me.

"I'll see you downstairs for rehearsal." I lowered my gaze and walked past her toward the stairs. I glanced back at her and noticed she had not moved. As much as I wanted to go back to her, I needed to give her the space she needed. I also needed to know that I was ready for this.

---

10

*F*riday rolled around and Deep Ember had a show that night at House of Blues. The tension between Penelope and I had been a bit thick. She thought I was still upset about her reaction to sleeping next to me. A part of me still was.

We pulled up in front of the building and it was still early. The show began at seven and we still had set up to do. The crew began to unload our equipment while we ventured inside. We took our place inside the green room while Chuck worked out last minute details. I grabbed a soda and took a swig.

"You'll go on at seven as planned," Chuck began then turned to me. "You ready, Kid?"

As many times as I have told him to stop calling me kid, I have accepted the fact to him, my nickname is Kid. Not his kid or anyone else's kid… just Kid. "Yeah, I'm cool." I took another drink and swallowed hard. The fizz burned in my throat and I coughed.

"You sure about that?" He raised a brow in concern.

"Yeah, I'm good." I took him by the arm and led him away from everyone else. I glanced over my shoulder and found Matt watching me. Always having my back, he's the best friend everyone could ever need. I gave him a nod, which he returned.

"Listen," I turned back to Chuck. "Keep the shit outta here as much as you can. I'm nervous and don't need the distractions of coke or anything else." I took another drink and finished the soda, then burped. "My bad."

"Whatever. I got your back, Kid, you know that." He winked and clapped my arm. "Trust me. Shit won't get back here unless I allow it back. Everyone knows the drill. Deep Ember is clean. Anyone caught is out and black listed."

I nodded and felt a sense of relief, but I would feel better once this was over. If Penelope was here, I think I would feel a bit better. She had this way of calming me... but I don't know what it is, exactly. I'm not sure if it's because she's become so familiar in my life, or if my addiction has turned to her. Hell, I wouldn't mind being addicted to her. I knew I could fuck that woman all damn day...

"Blaine?" Chuck's voice brought me out of my erotic thoughts. He never called me by my name unless it was important. "Don't be afraid to just leave if it becomes too much. We'll have you covered to leave."

I smiled. "Aww Chuck, you really DO care!"

"Fuck you, Kid." And like that, it's gone. I chuckled.

"Ah now, don't be that way! I was kidding!"

Chuck offered a few expletives then left the green room. I smiled and shook my head. The guys were sitting around the room, munching on the food and stretching their fingers. I decided to take a seat next to Matt. He would beat on his legs with his sticks. I assumed it was for him to warm up... that or he got off on pain.

"So," he turned to me, "what's the deal with you and Penelope?"

Wow, that took long enough for him to ask. "Dude, you were all up in my shit about Lexi. Now with Penelope, you're all casual and shit. What gives?"

"You didn't answer the question. Besides, you can't answer a question with a question, dumbass."

I grinned then shrugged. "Not much to say. I think she's fucking hot and I would like to date her, but she's going through some shit she needs to sort through." I raised a brow to his beating on his legs. "I don't want to be some rebound fuck."

Matt stopped and looked at me like I had two heads. "You don't want to be a rebound fuck?" The band stopped whatever they're all doing and all glance over. I looked around and shook my head.

"What?" I asked. "People can change. Fuck all y'all!"

Matt chuckled and I grinned. "Right. People change when they're sober. You're a damn asshole high, you know that?"

"So I've been told," I mumbled.

"I suppose the answer then," Matt started, "is that Penelope is not just a conquest. You really like her."

I nodded. "Matt," I glanced at him, "I've got it bad. I'm falling for her." I shook my head then leaned onto the couch to hold my head. "Trust me; I don't know what to do. I'm used to chicks just dropping everything to fuck me, suck me... hell, sometimes both at once. This? I don't know if I can do this."

"Wow," he started. "Hell, I don't know what to do with all... this," he motioned the area around me.

"What's that supposed to mean?" I asked.

"You're fucking pussy whipped!" Matt laughed at his own joke; one I didn't find humor in. I punched his shoulder. "What the fuck, man?"

"Shit's not funny, asshole."

He sighed. "Fine, you're really that into her?"

"Yeah. She makes me... feel things. I don't want anyone else. Hell, I don't even care to fuck some groupie tonight. I just want her here. I want her to watch and be there for me. I want her after we're done." I sighed and dropped my gaze. "She makes me want to be a better man."

"Well I wouldn't mind getting it on with someone tonight, maybe a few someones," Matt started.

"You'll have to be a better man up on the fucking stage, kid."
Chuck came back in the room with a couple of face mics. I stood
and walked over to him. He pinned one of the mic packs to my
pants then handed me the mouth piece. "Give'em hell, Kid," he
grinned. "And as far as the chick? They're on their way. I'll even
have her put on a cheer outfit for ya."

"Excellent!" Everything inside me lit up. Penelope is on her
way. She would be to the side, waiting for me. She would be who I
would go to, who I would be with.

"Yeah, want her in panties?" Chuck laughed.

"What?" It took me a minute to realize what he was referenc-
ing. "Oh... umm yeah, no panties would be fucking hot!"

"Fuck yeah, it would!" Matt offered.

"Oh, hell no!" I turned on my best friend. "Chuck, put her in
panties and long pants." I turned to look at my manager who
smiled like a kid who just found tits for the first time. "What the
fuck, man?"

"Nothing, Kid, you'll figure it out."

The crowd was huge. House of Blues didn't disappoint. I
caught myself glancing to the side of the stage in hopes of
catching a glimpse of Penelope, but she wasn't there. One of our
crowd favorite songs came up on the list to play. *The Way It Rolls
On.* Matt started his solo on the drums and immediately, the
crowd went fucking nuts. I couldn't help the smile I was giving.

Something caught my attention at the side of the stage and,
when I looked over, Penelope was there. My heart skipped a beat
and I grinned like a damn school boy. She waved and her outfit
didn't disappoint.

She had on a short... fucking short, black mini skirt that barely
covered what I most longed for between her legs. Fuck... if she
didn't have panties on... I felt my cock grow hard at the mere
thought. She wore a red halter-top that took her tits to a new level
of seduction. Her hair was pulled back into a messy bun and the
side of her head had new designs shaved in. What caught my eyes

the most was she looked like she had her legs decorated in diamond writing. I believe it is what Lexi used to call it bedazzling. "I'm with the band" was on one leg and "he is mine" was written on the other. I chuckled and she grinned when she realized I saw it.

Chuck walked up behind her and pointed at me to face the audience. For a moment, I'd forgotten where I was.

~

*T*he show ended three hours later. I was tired and drenched in sweat. I needed a shower, I needed water, and a very strong, very alive part of my head wanted coke. We were rushed back into the green room after the show and the cold of the air was a welcome relief.

"Fucking A! Did you see the fucking crowd tonight, man?" Matt yelled. Yeah, we were all still pretty deaf from the concert. I pulled off my mic set and put it on the table.

"Great skins tonight, man! You killed it!" I fist bumped him and grinned. "Fuck, I'm thirsty!"

"I got something for you." I turned to find Penelope entering the room. I smiled and made a beeline for her. "Oh no, you're gross and sweaty. Shower then hug." She handed over a bottle of water and stood there, staring up and down my body.

"Do you have any idea how inviting you look tonight? Holy FUCK, woman!" I opened the bottle and took a long pull on the water. After I swallowed hard, I shook my head. "Are you wearing panties? Please, tell me you're not wearing panties."

She leaned in and as she was about to answer me, the VIP group was ushered inside. Penelope smiled and took a step back. "I guess you'll just have to find out later." The women, and a few men, in the crowd pushed their way in and Penelope sidestepped out of the way. I noticed her smile falter slightly.

I had not been in this situation with her since we made out in my bed, she passed out, then I called her on her shit the next day... then kissed her. I wanted more. She knew it. I knew it. It was only a matter of time until one of us gave in to the temptation. I prayed it would be her. I wanted nothing more than to be her man... but not her rebound man.

"Blaine!" Women pushed at one another to get to me and my attention was torn away from my woman. One by one, people were taking pictures and I signed autographs. Hands were shoved in my pockets and numbers were left in their wake. Whispers of sexual innuendos were offered and all I could do was shake my head, no. I was afraid if I spoke, something like the bathroom incident with coke, possibly more, would occur.

I did not want to be put into a position of compromise. The last thing I needed was to be off with a few of the groupies and alone with coke or something worse. I glanced over at where Penelope stood and she was watching the crowd... not me. I'm not sure if what was occurring bothered her, but she knew the life of being in a band. She also knew the reputation I had... past tense. I don't want that life again.

Someone grabbed my elbow and pulled. I looked over and found a woman pulling me to the side. Her bottle blonde hair was straight and her make-up was a little too heavy. Her tits were obviously fake, since they were three times too big for her. She was so small and easily a double d. "I'll do whatever you want, anywhere you want, as long as you give me five minutes."

My brows raised in surprise. "Wow, how can I say no to that?" I chuckled and wrapped an arm around her shoulder. She snuggled in close. I didn't have the heart to tell her as soon as we rounded the corner, I would send her on her way to the security guards. One of her friends was apparently under the same impression and she snuggled into the other arm. This woman looked Asian with long black hair and legs up to her neck. At least her parts looked natural. I couldn't stand the feel of fake tits. Like fucking Rubbermaid dish bowls on the chest.

Chuck made an announcement that the VIP signing was wrapping up. Some complained, others turned, and began to leave. The women under my arms were pulling me to get going.

I started to pull my arms away when the women took a hold of my waist.

"Where you going, baby?" the blonde asked me. Her friend giggled and rubbed her hand over my crotch.

"Whoa! Okay wild things, let's get outta here." I lead them toward the door and when I glanced over at Penelope to mouth *I'll be right back*, but all I saw was her... leaving.

"Fuck!" I yelled out.

"That's exactly what we intend to do," the Asian girl informed me.

"Right, well let's do it, then." I walked them around the corner of the green room to the designated *do something with these sluts* area. I pulled my arms away and took their hands. "Now listen to me ladies. You are not getting lucky with me tonight. Instead," I looked up to the guard, "Tito here is going to escort you out and offer you ladies a ride home."

"Aww, no!" the blonde woman yelled. "We want you, Blaine! Come on!"

"Yeah, I have coke!" the Asian announced. That's all I needed to know before I lost my shit.

"Get the FUCK out. Now!" I released their hands and stepped back. They stared at me; slack jawed. "Did I fucking stutter? Get the FUCK out!"

"You heard the man," Tito answered. At least I thought his name was Tito. He was a huge man that was bald and looked like he stepped off the Mafia train.

"I'm clean, and have been clean. Who are you to bring that shit in here?" I shook my head and walked back into the green room. It was almost empty, save for Matt making out on the couch with a groupie chick. He was going to get lucky. Good for you, fucker.

"Where did Penelope go?" I asked anyone who would answer. Chuck turned and looked me over.

"What the fuck happened? What just went down?"

"What do you mean?" I looked around his shoulder and as I was about to pass, he grabbed me.

"What the fuck happened? I see it on your face. What happened?"

"Some groupies came in and thought they were going to get lucky because they brought coke."

"They fucking what?" Chuck's face went red. "I had them all fucking checked!" He took off for whoever was doing back check. Someone was about to eat it. "She took off that way, Penny did," Chuck said over his shoulder as he pointed in her departure direction.

I pulled out my phone and called her. It rang once then went to voicemail. I hung up and called again. Voicemail.

"Dammit Penelope, answer your phone. I didn't do anything with the fucking groupies. Come on!" I hung up and began to text her.

Please call me back!

"I'll go," Derek offered.

"Why?" I glanced over to him with a curious gaze. "Why would you?"

"Because you didn't do shit. She probably took off because of what I said anyway." He dropped his gaze to the floor.

"What?" I hit end then shoved my phone in my pocket. I grabbed him by his shirt and threw him up against the wall. Apparently, this is all that was needed to break Matt from his lip lock. "What the fuck did you tell her?"

"I… I told her to cut her losses. That once a fuck, always a fuck. It's to be expected with musicians and shit doesn't change." Derek looked from me to whoever was beside me, most likely Matt.

"Why the FUCK would you do that? WHY?" I got in his face and screamed.

"Because! You're fucking Blaine from Deep Ember! You fuck'em and leave'em after every fucking show! Why should this be different! She's fucking Penelope man! She's like my fucking sister!" Derek began shaking in my hands. "I fucking love her man!"

"Wait, what?" I asked. "You're in love with her?"

"No, that's not what I fucking said. I said I love her. If you can't fucking tell, dude, I'm fucking gay, alright? I love that woman like a sister. I have a thing for dudes. I like dick. Trust me; I don't want her like that."

"You're gay?" Matt asked him.

"Yeah, why?" Derek stared between the both of us looking scared to death. I was a big guy, but Matt... Matt was fucking huge and covered in tattoos.

Matt chuckled. "Dude, I had no idea. You could've fooled me."

"Why? Because I don't act gay or wear frilly things?"

"No, because you have never let on otherwise. Dude," Matt held his arms out. "Gay men love me. Don't know what it is, but I'm like a gay magnet."

I let go of Derek, the heat and rage inside of me simmering down. At the turn of events, I honestly wanted to laugh. I had no idea Derek was gay, but it explained a lot.

The way he was overprotective of Penelope but never let on he was attracted to her. The way he would watch us when we played, almost eyeing us like candy. And now... I glanced at Matt then back at Derek. I laughed and shook my head.

"What?" Matt asked me.

"He's looking at you like you're candy, man." I glanced over at Derek and he blushed.

"See?" Matt grinned. "Told ya. Gay man magnet."

"That should be your super hero name," Derek offered with a

chuckle. "Now," he turned back to me, "Let me go find Penelope and I'll tell her it was all a misunderstanding."

I nodded and clapped his shoulder. "Thanks Derek. And next time, don't interfere. I respect and understand why you did, but this thing between me and Penelope, it's real. Let it happen."

Derek nodded and pushed off the wall. "Seriously, I'm very sorry." He glanced at Matt again and grinned. "Too bad you don't bat for my team."

"Umm..." Matt was speechless. He lowered his gaze and rubbed the back of his neck with his hand. Chuck came back into the green room cussing to himself. I watched him as he grabbed a beer from the cooler and opened it. He downed probably half of it then walked past us, still cussing. Obviously, something happened and when he was like this, it was best to leave him alone.

"I'll follow Derek and see if he convinces her to come back. If he can't, I'll see what I can do." Matt glanced at the woman on the couch he was making out with and shrugged slightly. "I'll be back," she nodded and smiled. "Stay here, don't leave," he told the girl. She smiled and nodded then Matt left the green room.

Hell had broken lose around me. My heart pounded in my chest and it ached. If Penelope thought I would actually fuck those groupies... I sighed, sat down on one of the chairs, and held my head in my hands. I glanced over to the woman Matt was making out with and she smiled at me.

I took another drink of my water then sat back in my chair. How the fuck did this happen? Is this karma kicking me in the ass for all the shit I pulled when I was high? I took another drink of water and closed my eyes, picturing Penelope in my mind. Her smile, her laugh... anything to distract me from her leaving.

11

*M*att ran down the hall and found Derek talking to her. It didn't look to be going very well. He waited for a moment before stepping in.

"Penelope! Hold up!"

"Why?" she turned on him and glared. "Why should I? So you can tell me that Blaine isn't running off with those... those whores? Why should this be any different than any other time?" She turned around, her back to Matt. "I guess I should have known. Maybe I'm stupid, but I honestly thought he cared for me."

"Maybe you are stupid," Matt started and Penelope quickly turned on him. "No, woman, I'm serious. If you had stayed back and waited, you would have seen him come back empty handed. There's a green room we take the groupies to we have no intentions of being with. Chuck set this up for us a few years ago."

"And I'm supposed to believe you, because you're his best friend, right?" She held her hand up and shook her head. "I'm not buying it. I'm not a stranger to this life, Matt. I know what goes on behind the scenes."

"No, I don't think you really do." Matt stepped closer to her and crossed his arms over his chest. "Do you have any idea how hard he struggles, day to day? Do you have a clue to how much shit he put up with when he finally sobered up? He's the front man for our band. Temptation is everywhere, especially with you."

She flinched and stepped back. "What the fuck is that supposed to mean?"

Derek watched the two of them argue then took a step back. He leaned against the wall and watched the interaction between Penelope and Matt unfold.

"A man with an addiction issue will usually transition said addiction to something else." He raised a single brow as if willing a punch line for a joke he just told. "Dammit Penelope, don't you get it?"

"Apparently not," she told him. "How do his addiction issues have anything to do with me? I'm not a drug nor am I alcohol."

Matt shook his head. "Just think about it for a minute. Maybe it'll come to you."

She shook her head. "No. There's no way he's addicted to me, or the idea of being addicted to me, Matt. We've been through some stuff together, but honestly, what we had was real."

"Really? Then why are you walking away if it's so real?"

"Matt!" Derek's voice echoed slightly as he yelled. "Lay off her. This is my fault."

Penelope looked past Matt's shoulder and raised her eyebrows. "Derek? What do you mean?"

"Stop," Derek interrupted her question. "Don't leave."

"Why? You told me where Blaine was going. Why should I wait?"

"Because," Derek looked between Penelope and Matt, then back at her, "because I may have embellished a little." He held together his index and thumb with a little space in-between.

Penelope glared at him then looked at Matt. "Go away. I need to talk to my lead singer."

Matt chuckled. "Yeah, I'll go away when you see reason. You

send my best friend off into a drug binge; you get to sit with him." Matt turned to give them space to talk and leaned against the far wall.

Penelope shook her head. "Whatever. Now," she looked at Derek. "Explain."

Derek sighed and went into the details of Blaine not leaving with the women, that he had lied to protect her. He held his gaze down and refused to look at Penelope. "Penny, I feel like shit; I'm so sorry."

"Why Derek? Why would you do that?"

"I was afraid of him hurting you. I couldn't stand the thought of you being turned like one of his many door knob whores."

Her eyes widened and something between shock and anger touched her features. "You had no right to make that decision for me, Derek. No right!"

He nodded and shifted in his step. "I'm sorry, I truly am." His voice dropped into a softer tone. "Please, Penny I'm so sorry."

"I can't... I can't do this."

"Oh, so his word is gold, but mine isn't?" Matt called to her. "Whatever." He pushed off the wall and began heading back toward the green room.

"I need time away," Penelope told Derek. "I need to... I don't know; get myself together. I just need time away from this. I've been single for five minutes and I feel like I just let Blaine down. Hell, he's not my boyfriend but he's done more for me than my ex ever did."

Derek nodded and slowly, looked up at her. "Will you ever forgive me? I'm so sorry."

She caught his gaze and offered a small smile. "You're like a brother to me. Of course, I forgive you for looking out for me." Derek smiled and went in to hug her when Penelope held her hand up. "Oh, Derek, I'm not done. I forgive you, but the act? No way. You have some serious making up to do. You can start by telling our production manager, Blaine, I'm taking a few weeks to myself. I don't know when I'll be back but I need to be left alone. Understand?" With that, Penelope turned and left Derek standing there alone.

"Penelope? Please don't go."

"Too late. I'm gone." She turned the corner and left Derek standing there alone.

He lowered his gaze and turned back toward the direction of the green room. He glanced up and saw Matt watching him from the distance. He knew he was in trouble and it was a matter of seconds before the wrath of what he had done was unleashed upon him. Blaine and Chuck had every right to fire him for his meddling. As much as he could tell himself they wouldn't get rid of the lead singer, he thought of Blaine.

All the drama and the drug use he put his band through... yet he's still here. He sighed and shook his head. The walk back was long and his stomach became nervous. He glanced up at Matt as he closed the distance.

"She's, umm... taking some time away." Derek glanced past Matt and found me standing in the room; mouth slack jawed.

"She actually left?" I asked. Derek nodded then slipped past Matt to face Chuck.

"You fucked up, kid." Chuck crossed his arms over his chest and watched him for a moment. "But nothing we can't recover from."

"Really?" Derek asked with a little excitement in his voice.

"Really. You know all the shit this fucker caused me?" He pointed at me. "Hell, this is nothing."

"Hey!" I yelled. "I'm not in the room or anything."

"Good thing we're good on recording for now. Hell, we can focus on song writing for a while." Chuck looked to me and raised a brow. "Weren't you working on a song?"

I nodded. "Yeah, it was with Penelope. I'm sure I can finish it. I hope I can." My body shook, visibly. I needed air. I needed something to take the edge off. I needed Penelope. I gritted my teeth and left the room. We had decided to stay at the hotel near House of Blues tonight. It became custom to do so in prevention of psycho fans from following us home on our own turf. I stood and headed back toward my suite.

"Kid?" Chuck called.

"I'm fine," I called back. "I'll be fine."

❧

The driver dropped me off at my hotel and I ventured inside. I had a private entrance that allowed me to bypass the front lobby, thus avoiding any late night groupie confrontations. I pressed the button for the elevator and waited. I pulled my phone out and stared at the blank screen. No messages. No Penelope.

The doors opened and I stepped inside. I pressed my floor button and leaned against the wall. The elevator began moving up and I stared at the numbers as they climbed to the penthouse. The doors opened at my floor and I stepped inside. The entire area belonged to me tonight and I'd had every intention on sharing it with Penelope.

The fragrant smell of fresh flowers touched my senses. I glanced into the open bedroom at the petals spread across the bed. I kept walking and didn't want to step foot inside. I needed a shower. I needed to get the events of tonight washed off my body. If I scrubbed hard enough, maybe the pain would offer some sort of relief. I decided to take my shower in the guest bathroom. Fuck the master bedroom. Not tonight.

As I stepped past the kitchen area, something shiny caught my peripheral vision. I glanced over at a silver bucket holding iced champagne. Making a beeline for the cold alcohol, I yanked it from the container. Ice fell to the floor and chilled water streamed down my hand.

I pushed the cork off and it fizzed and poured over my hand. I lifted it to my lips and came within an inch of my mouth. I hesitated and my chest heaved with the breath in my lungs. It foamed over the lip of the bottle and I felt it touch my chin. I didn't move... I couldn't. I couldn't do it; I couldn't drink. Not now. Not after all this time.

I sighed and lowered my arm. A low growl that became louder and louder erupted from me. I stared at the bottle in my hand then looked at the contents on the floor.

Another day and time, I would have claimed alcohol abuse. I would have licked the contents from the floor. I wouldn't have cared who watched. Like coke, wherever it was, my nose was there.

A long sigh left my lips and I wanted to collapse on the floor. Everything I had been working toward had suddenly been taken from me. This time I felt like the victim rather than the antagonist. I had never understood how badly I hurt the people around me until this moment. Now? Yeah, now, I knew.

I poured the contents, what was left in the bottle, down the drain. I don't even want to know how much this shit cost. It would be on my bill and I would send it to Chuck. He would pay it as he always did. Unless furniture was broken, we have an undocumented agreement there would be no questions asked.

I stepped through the liquid on the floor and slipped. I fell hard on my ass and yelled when my elbow hit the tile. "MOTHER FUCKER!" I yelled as loud as I could. Anyone within earshot would have heard me, but I couldn't give a shit. Let them come.

As I rolled to my hands and knees, my palms rested in the cold liquid. I stared at it and, suddenly, I was parched. I felt my elbows bend as I began lowering my face toward the glorious liquid. I needed this escape. I needed this moment, this clarity of the evening. I deserved it. I've been good for how long?

"No!" I turned my face away. The demon inside coaxed me into looking back. The alcohol was like oxygen and I needed it to survive, didn't I?

I closed my eyes and shifted my weight to my hip. Resting my elbow on my knee, I sat there and stared across the room. I almost lost it that night in the club and Penelope stayed with me. Tonight, she's nowhere to be found and more than ever, I need her. How the fuck did I become this... person?

After disposing of the empty bottle and getting to my feet, I headed toward the guest room and stripped out of my clothes. The guest bedroom was brown in décor with a dark, chocolate brown bedspread. Pictures of trees and parks decorated the walls. It was almost depressing. Making my way toward the bathroom, I turned on the shower. I looked at myself in the mirror and stared into my own eyes, then at the tattoos on my body. I remember all the ink I'd gotten and why I'd gotten it, even the Latin one I lied to Lexi about. "Lexi..." I sighed and dropped my head down. "I need to call her."

I stepped into the shower to clean up from tonight's events and eventually, head to bed... alone. Penelope was on my mind and it caused my heart to almost ache to consider sleeping with someone else. Even the fact that she had considered it... thank you, Derek... hurt a lot.

I sighed as the hot water streamed over my head. Every time I closed my eyes, I saw her. I wanted more than anything to have her here with me now, but alas, that would not happen... and maybe not ever.

The brown room called for me and I was exhausted. Soon, sleep would take me under. Soon, I would forget all about my broken heart and Penelope... at least until the sun woke me.

12

The next morning I woke with the sun as it shone through a crack in the curtains. It whispered across my face, almost teasing me. I groaned and rolled to my side. The brown room came into view... and with it, memories of last night.

"Fuck this," I mumbled to myself. First thing to do is leave this damn hotel. I was not sticking around for a *woe is me* party without Penelope. She wanted to leave? Fine. Let her go. "Yeah right," I told myself. I wanted her... no, needed her in my life. I knew it. I was just too much of an asshole to admit to anyone, especially myself.

I called down to the front desk to have my bags tended to and to have my driver ready. I wanted to go home. I needed the comforts of my own walls, even if it was just my bedroom. Maybe I'll call home and talk to someone familiar.

Lexi...

I sighed and dropped my head down. I owed her a huge apology. Same with her husband. I hated using that word with her, but it is what it is. I not only lost her, hell, I pushed her out the door and into his arms.

I pushed my sunglasses onto my face and pulled on a Texas

Rangers baseball hat. I might live in Boulder, but I was still a diehard Rangers fan. Wearing a fitted dark grey t-shirt and old, ratty looking jeans, I made my way down to the lobby. As I stepped outside, I found my driver waiting just outside the limo. He was never late and never disappointed.

As I made my way over, I'm not sure if he recognized me or if the baseball hat gave it away, but he opened the back passenger door for me. "Mr. Blaine. Pleasure to see you."

I simply nodded and slid into the car. He shut the door and I stared out the one-way tinted glass. When I was high and drunk, I would hang out the window for my fans. Sometimes I would hang onto them while we kissed... Now? I slumped down in the seat and waited for my home to come into view.

~

*W*e pulled into the circular drive of my home and I opened my door. My driver lifted my bag from the trunk and set it on the ground. I thanked him and grabbed hold of the bags as I walked inside. He took the car back to what I assumed was the hotel.

I made my way upstairs and set my bags on the bed. Unzipping the first one, I sorted through the contents and put away my clean clothes. Everything else, I threw to the floor for washing. I would deal with them later.

Taking a seat on my bed, I laid back, and stared at my ceiling. "I fucked up things with Lexi, then with Penelope. I'm just a bona fide genius." I groaned and laid my arm across my eyes. The blackness did nothing but remind me what Penelope looked like. Her perfect body lit up the darkness behind my eyelids. Her perfect tits... the way they would sit in her bra or her corset. Her long, slender legs... how long I've imagined them wrapped around my waist when we would finally have sex.

"Fuck," I mumbled. My hand rubbed across my cock as it hardened in my pants. I didn't want blue balls but I didn't want to jerk it off, either. I wanted Penelope. I needed her in more ways than for just a good fuck. I needed her in my life. I also knew I needed to let her go to find herself... or what the hell ever she was trying to do.

"Hell, maybe I need this, too," I told myself. I sat up and my bedroom phone caught my gaze. I shook my head. "Bitch would drop dead if she knew I wanted to call her." I sighed and picked up my phone then dialed the last known number I had for Lexi.

"Hello?" Her mother answered the phone. It had been years since I'd spoken with Mrs. Griffin. She would probably hang up on me, but here goes nothing.

"Hi, Mrs. Griffin? It's Blaine."

There was a pause on the other end. I hoped I didn't cause the woman to have a heart attack.

"Before you hang up on me," I started, "I'm calling to apologize." She sighed into the phone and I heard her clear her throat.

"Apologize for what, exactly? Treating my daughter like shit? Threatening to take my farm? Oh is there something else you did, like sleep with her best friend?"

My head dropped between my shoulders. "Yeah, I deserve that. And this is why I'm calling, to apologize for all of that... and so much more," I sighed. "Mrs. Griffin, I don't deserve it but please, I'm asking you to forgive me. I promise, I'm not asking for anything in return. I just... I'm trying to right my wrongs."

She laughed into the receiver, although there was no humor in it. "And you just expect us to put behind everything you did and say, 'Okay Blaine, all is forgiven?'"

"No, not at all. I expect you to do nothing but understand I'm asking for your forgiveness for what I did. I was wrong and I know that. I was a different person then."

"Oh, and you're different now? Please, humor me." The sarcasm was heavy in her voice.

I explained to my ex-fiancé's mother about my drug addiction detox, my recovery, and how long I have been clean. I told her how I have put myself into my music. "I probably fucked up the next best thing that walked into my life, aside from your daughter."

"Son, I'll not have you use that language with me."

"I'm sorry, Mrs. Griffin, I didn't mean any offense. If it's not too much to ask, I'm hoping you'd have Lexi give me a call. I have a number for her, but I'm sure it's changed."

"You're damn straight it changed. No, I will not give it to you."

"I didn't ask, Mrs. Griffin." I sighed into the phone. "Look, I just want to tell her, and Robert both, how sorry I am."

"What is your PR number? I'll have hers call yours. Good enough?"

"Yes, ma'am; I would appreciate that very much. Matter of fact, just have her PR rep call me directly." I provided her my number.

"Alright, Blaine, I'll do that. But Blaine?"

I could hear the hesitation in her voice. "Yes, Mrs. Griffin?"

"If you're being honest with me here, I'm glad you're making an effort. There are a lot of children out there that look up to you. Give them a good idol to look up to."

"Yes, ma'am, I'm definitely working on that." I smiled into the phone and knew if I ever gained forgiveness from this woman, this would be it. "Thank you."

Mrs. Griffin hung up the phone. Now I waited. Who knew how long that wait would be and who knew if Mrs. Griffin would even make the damn call, but I had to hope that she would. Needing to gain the forgiveness of my first love, well, it was a start.

My next call would be to Abby Masters. I'd fucked this woman around so many times, and in so many ways. Because of me, she'd lost her friendship with Lexi. Well, she was part of that too, but mainly, it was me. She loved the attention I gave her and I took advantage of that... in a very bad way.

I sighed and scrolled through the numbers stored in my

phone. Maybe Abby still had the same digits, but I might be fooling myself in thinking so. I found her name and pulled it up on my screen. What would I say to her? What would she say to me? Whatever it was, I probably deserved it. I pressed dial and watched my phone connect.

"Hello?" Her voice came through and I stared at it for a moment. I am seldom left speechless but what the hell do I say? "Hello?"

I quickly brought the phone to my ear and blinked. "Umm, Abby?"

"Yes?" she answered. "Who is this?"

I sighed and closed my eyes, getting myself ready for whatever onslaught attack she would provide. "It's Blaine."

The phone went silent and I waited... "Abby?"

"Well, I thought for certain you'd probably died when you OD'd and I'll be honest, a part me WISHED you had!"

"Okay, I deserved that..."

"Oh, you fucker, I'm not done!" She cut me off and continued reading me the riot act. She hated me and it was clear. When she told me how Lexi punched her in public and basically kicked her ass, I closed my eyes, and shook my head.

"Abby, I'm trying to call to say I'm sorry. I'm not calling to rub anything in. Please understand..."

"No, you motherfucker! You don't get to call and say you're sorry for what you did! You used me and made me look like a damned fool and a damned slut!"

I sighed and let her vent. I pulled the phone away at one point and allowed her to continue. When her voice quieted down, I put the phone back and gave her another few seconds.

"Are you done?" I asked.

"That all depends on what you really want from me."

"Nothing, Abby. I want nothing other than to apologize to you. You're right about everything. I'm sorry and that's all I wanted to say."

"Wait." Her tone changed from angry to bitter. "Someone got to you, didn't they? They hurt you and now you're feeling it from the other end. Holy shit, someone fucked you and left you high and dry, huh?"

"Say what you want, woman, but it's not like that."

"Oh I think it's very much like that. Whatever, Blaine. Get out of my life; I hate you." She disconnected the call. I stared at my phone and shook my head. Tossing it on my bed, I laid back and sighed. What's that saying; you can lead a horse to water but can't make it drink? Well, consider the horse led.

My phone chimed. When I glanced, I saw a text message. I swiped my finger and found Abby's name.

You hurt me bad, Blaine. Really bad. It'll take more than a phone call to let that go. Maybe in time... I don't know... maybe we can talk but right now, I can't. Good luck with your recovery.
Abby

I set my phone down without replying to her. What would I say? Thank you? Not likely. I stood and began making my way toward my bedroom door when my phone rang. Likely, it would be Abby calling me back; it also could be Robert's PR firm. There is no way I could get in touch, directly, with a Senator's wife.

I took a chance and grabbed my cell. Well, it wasn't Abby but I did recognize the area code as Dallas. I answered the call. "Hello?" Suddenly, my stomach felt nervous.

"Blaine?" The male's voice was familiar but I couldn't quite place it.

"Yeah, this is Blaine."

"This is Robert. We got your message."

My heart hammered in my chest from nerves. I wasn't expecting Robert, but hell, it was a start. "Hey man, how're you doing?"

"Cut the shit, Blaine. What do you want? Lexi's mom called us. She said you phoned offering an apology. What are you after?"

"I see politics has done wonders for your speech making," I told him sarcastically.

"Excuse me?"

"Nothing. Look, something has happened and honestly, I've had a moment of clarity. It's not often I do this, so take it or leave it."

"Clarity? Look, if you're calling in an effort to make a play..."

"Stop," I interrupted him, "I'm calling to apologize, and that is all."

"Apologize? For what exactly?" he asked. "The last time we saw you, you were at my inaugural ball. You weren't exactly invited and you made Lexi uncomfortable."

"Yeah, I know." I slumped on my bed and stared across the room. "I've been a real dick and I'm... well hell, man, I'm sorry. That's why I called Mrs. Griffin. I'm sorry for what I put Lexi through, I'm sorry for being such a dick to you, hell, I even called Abby and apologized."

There was silence for a moment then, surprising me, Robert chuckled. "You called Abby?" he laughed again. "How did that go over?"

"Umm," I paused for a moment, not real sure how to take him laughing, but went with it. "Not good. The word mother fucker was used often."

Robert chuckled again. "Well, it's deserved. Look, if we're being honest here, Lexi has long since been over you. She's moved on and we're happily married. She's started up her own equine clinic and usually works the track.

"I can't believe I'm about to offer this, but if you want to talk to her, I'll go get her." Robert sighed into the phone. "I don't like this, not one bit, but something tells me you're being sincere."

"I am. I met someone and she's helped me in ways Lexi never

could. Not that I ever let her, anyway. She thinks I did things behind her back."

"What things? Honestly, that sounds a little childish."

"Yeah… She thinks I fucked two women after my concert."

"Isn't that your thing, though? I mean, because with Lexi, you…"

I cut him off. "Yeah, I know I did that to her, but no it's not like that. Not this time."

"What happened then, that she thinks you did?"

"Look, as much as I want to reminisce with you, my quarrel is not with you, it's with Lexi. If I could talk to her, please…" I trailed off and decided not to say anything else. Robert would allow me to speak with her, or he wouldn't.

"Blaine, I've been here listening the entire time." Lexi's voice chimed in and I quickly sat up straight. "It's okay, baby, you can hang up." The phone clicked once.

"You were listening in?" I asked.

"Yep," she told me. "Now Blaine, what is this I hear about an apology?"

I took a deep breath and began. "Lexi, I'm so sorry for everything I ever put you through. I was in a bad place and I'm not using it as an excuse. I'm just asking for your forgiveness."

"What changed?" She asked.

"I've met someone while I've been sober. Seeing things… like this… clearly… it's been eye opening. She makes me want to be a better man."

"Wow," she offered. "Umm…" She paused a moment then continued. "Blaine, what is it about her that makes you feel this way?"

I shook my head. "Honestly? I don't know. I mean, she's been there when I needed her and when she broke things off with her boyfriend…"

"Wait," She interrupted me, "she has a boyfriend?"

"Had," I clarified. "She broke up with him."

"Because of you?"

"His perception was part of the reason."

"Did you ever give him a reason to suspect your intentions?"

I knew where she was going with this. "Lexi, Penelope knew how I felt about her."

"You made your confession while she was still with her man? Blaine, that's cold."

"No, yes, no. Wait," I stopped to gather my thoughts. I hadn't actually considered this yet and I was shocked to be having this conversation with my ex. "She knew I liked her, but it wasn't until after they broke up that I made my intentions clear."

"Did you give her time to recover from her break up?"

"How much time would she need? She wasn't with the guy that much and hell, she broke up with him."

"Blaine, seriously? You broke my heart and stomped on it. You were my first... everything. It took a lot to get over you, definitely more than just a second."

"Lexi, I'm so sorry." I wasn't sure what else to say.

"I forgive you." Her voice was soft and if the background noise was any louder, I'm afraid I would have missed it.

"Why?" I asked. "I mean, thank you, but why?"

"I can hear it in your voice that you're sincere and this woman means a lot to you." She paused and I'm sure she was waiting for something in return. I opened my mouth to reply, when she continued. "Blaine, I'm only curious. What does this Penelope have that I didn't? Why her?"

"Lexi, there's no comparison."

"Ouch, you asshole." she huffed and I imagined her rolling her eyes.

"Oh damn, that's not how I meant it."

"How DID you mean it then?"

"Well, with you, I was high... a lot. I didn't care. I knew you would be there, if and when I needed you. You were like a familiar comfort. With Penelope, I'm sober and I'm seeing things differently." I sighed and continued. "I know this hurts to hear and I'm so sorry, but I'll be honest with you. If I had never dabbled into drugs, it would be you." I lowered my voice to a whisper. "It's always been you."

Silence enveloped the phone for a few minutes. I heard Lexi sniff and I imagined she was wiping tears. "Blaine, give her time. She'll come around. If she feels the same way for you, she'll come back. Sober, you're quite the catch. You're kind and generous. I remember that part of you. That was the part of you I fell in love with and, if she can't see that, then she doesn't deserve you."

As I was about to retort… to the most amazing 'I forgive you' speech, she hung up the phone. A tear slipped down my cheek and I quickly swiped it away. I never, in this lifetime anyway, thought I would have the forgiveness of my first love. However, in this lifetime, I wanted…I needed Penelope to be my last love.

I was in love with her. I knew it. She knew it. Time? I could do that. I just hoped that it worked and she would come back. The realist in me knew she would; she was under contract and had no choice, unless she wanted to be replaced. The other side, the emotional one, wanted her to come back on her own accord. I wanted her in my arms and wanted to kiss her. I needed her to be in my life.

I quickly made my way downstairs and went into my study. Shutting the door behind me, I picked up the words Penelope and I had started writing. Feeling inspired, I wrote a few words down.

I'm standing outside your door
Desperately needing a fix
Of your arms around me
Oh that intoxicating mix
The way you calm my fears
The way you dry my tears

My pain consumes me

The demons laugh in vain
They taunt me to fall into their plight
To give up on life
I fall to my knees
Praying please

Bring me back from the brink
You're my missing link
Lay down beside me
Hold me through the dark of night
Stop the fright
And heal me with your touch

I stared at the words for a moment and considered their meaning. I needed a fix and the fix was her... not drugs, not alcohol. I set the pencil down and ran my hand through my hair. I didn't want to see her as an addiction. I needed her as my woman, my partner in this hell called life. I sighed and sat back in my chair as I went over the words to the song again.

A light tap sounded on the door to my study brought me from my thoughts. "I don't want to be disturbed right now." I assumed it was one of my guys. If it were Chuck, he would have barged in, no knocking. Whoever it was tapped on the door again. "I said, go away!"

"Blaine?" It was Penelope's voice. My heart hammered in my chest and in seconds, I made it to the study door. I pulled it open and found her, the love of my new life standing directly in front of me. I wanted to smile. I wanted to kiss her.

"Penelope..."

13

"*P*enelope? How long have you been here?"

"Long enough, I suppose." She dropped her gaze and leaned against the wall. "I watched you walk from your room down to the study. I've been here a while. Your staff allowed me in this morning." She glanced up at me and her eyes appeared to glisten.

"I've been doing a lot of thinking. I think we really need to talk," I told her.

She nodded. "I agree." Penelope took in a deep breath then she raised her eyes to mine. They were a cloudy blue, troubled. "I have a lot to say and need to say it. If I don't, I might chicken out."

"Let's go down to the studio. It's quiet. No one is here but us. If you want to scream," I shrug, "no one will hear you."

"Why would I want to scream?" She asked in confusion.

I grinned. "Why not? Maybe you'll scream my name." I winked at her and turned back toward my study.

"Blaine, this isn't the time for a joke."

"I know that." I glanced back over my shoulder as I grabbed the words to the song. "I only wanted to lift the mood. Come on, I have something to show you anyway."

"I really need to tell you a few things, though."

"And you will. Let's go." I led her downstairs to the recording area and closed the door behind us. Usually, I never locked it but something told me that I should. It clicked into place. Penelope stood and stared at me. Her face was haunted and I could tell whatever was bothering her, it was eating her alive inside.

I stepped closer and decided to hug her. My arms pulled her in close. She didn't move. "Penelope..."

"Blaine, please," she whispered.

Reluctantly, I let her go and stared into her beautiful eyes. Her hair was pulled back into a messy bun and her tank top hugged her body. The cut off shorts were just an added bonus.

"Come on." We walked into the recording room where Mongrels of Soul's instruments laid in wait. Her bass shined from the light and Penelope strolled over to it. She gently ran her fingers across the top of it. "What's on your mind?" I asked her.

"I came back here last night, after I left. I had hoped you would have returned here." She glanced over at me and continued. "Matt and Derek both found me last night, told me what you did."

"Okay," I started and she shook her head.

"It's not that easy here, Blaine. In my head, I knew... I just knew you were fucking them." She looked back at her guitar and simply stared at it. "It continued to nag at me, relentlessly."

"Penelope, but I didn't..."

"Blaine, dammit, stop talking!" She rounded on me and glared in my direction. "Let me finish."

I sat back against the seat Joe used for drumming. I crossed my arms over my chest and waited for her to continue.

"When you weren't here, I drove to the hotel. I went as far as asking the front desk for your room." She shrugged. "Unfortunately, or maybe fortunately for you, they wouldn't give it out. I had half a mind to ask Chuck or Matt for your room number, but I didn't want to appear desperate or give the impression we were fucking."

I had no idea she had come back here or even ventured to the hotel period. She came back for me and I wasn't here. Fuck my life. I pinched the bridge of my nose and lowered my head. The room was silent for a moment, at least until I heard her whimper.

When I looked up, she had turned her back to me. Her body shook slightly as she sobbed. Now, I felt like shit. She thought I threw everything away on two whores and, after being told I was alone, she couldn't find me.

I closed the distance to her and touched her shoulders. "Penelope," I whispered her name and leaned my chin on her shoulder. "I was at the hotel last night. I wish I had known. Please, please understand I'm right here, right now."

She nodded and turned around. I pulled her close and held her while she cried. I rubbed her back and cupped her head. "I finished your song."

Penelope sniffed and looked up. Her eyes were red from her tears and she blinked. "You... you did?" I nodded. "Can I hear it?"

"Yes. I would like to record you singing it. Tonight."

"What? I can't... I don't know how it goes. I don't think..."

"No thinking, just singing. I wrote it, I just need you to read it then sing the words how you feel it happen. Can you do that?"

"It's so... raw like that."

I nodded. "Exactly." I smiled at her and lifted her chin up slightly. "Would you do this for me?"

She stared into my eyes for a moment. No words had passed. Nobody moved. She stayed in my arms and our bodies pressed against each other.

I'm not sure who gave in first, but the next moment, we were kissing. Her arms pulled me closer as they wrapped around my back. My hands cupped her face and my tongue swept across her lips. She opened them for me and my tongue sought hers.

Penelope surprised me and pushed against my body. I wasn't sure where we were headed until a chair hit the back of my knees.

I fell into it and pulled her onto my lap. She straddled me and pressed her hands on my shoulders.

"You have too many clothes on," she whispered.

I growled against her lips. "I can easily remedy that." I tugged against the hem of her tank top and lifted it over her head. She had on a black satin bra that was thinly lined. Fuck me; she was sexy.

Fisting my hand in her hair, I tugged and pulled her head back, exposing her neck. I kissed down her throat to her chest. My free hand grasped one of her breasts and I grinned. "I didn't think it was right to bring this up, but that nipple ring is sexy as hell." I felt her ring on my palm and looked down. I pulled her bra to the side and exposed her pierced nipple. I raised a brow and glanced up at her. She smirked and pressed my face into her breast. My tongue licked around her piercing and I flicked it. She hissed in pleasure and allowed her head to fall back.

I unfastened her bra and pulled it off her body. Exposing her breasts, I ran my tongue over each nipple then gently blew against the wet skin. She gasped and held into my arms.

Penelope righted herself and pressed me against the chair. She pulled at my shirt until it was over my head. Her eyes moved over my chest and her fingers lightly traced the tattoos. Her eyes met mine and she quickly kissed me again.

I reached between us and began unbuttoning my pants. She sat up enough so I could push them down. Penelope lowered herself back down and began to grind against me. I groaned and gripped her ass in my hands.

"Fuck woman," I mumbled against her lips. She whimpered then nibbled softly on my bottom lip.

"Blaine," she whispered my name and pulled away just enough to look into my eyes. "I need you."

Holding her close, I stood and kept her legs wrapped around my waist. Penelope barely weighed anything in my arms. She kissed me again as I started to walk across the room.

"I need to see," I chuckled. She grinned and went for my ear. She sucked on my lobe and she nibbled on the skin just under it. I made it as far as the couch in the room and laid her on it.

Hovering above her, I worked on removing her shorts and panties. Penelope was naked in my arms and damn, was she beautiful. The tattoo I saw that night in my room snaked around her waist, just under her breasts. After this, I planned on taking a better look. As for right now, she is mine.

I kissed her again and grinded against her folds. She was wet and she wanted this as much as I did. I didn't think, I didn't consider, I just acted on instinct.

Reaching between us, I grabbed my cock and pressed it against her, then pushed inside. Her back arched and she moaned. I pulled back and thrust into her. I moaned into her neck as she gasped.

"I'm not hurting you, am I?" I asked her. I slowed my rhythm down and teased her by barely moving back and forth. She started moving underneath me, trying to get more friction.

"Fuck no, I need you!" Penelope gripped my back under my arms and dug her nails in. "Fuck me!"

I sat up and did as she asked. I pulled back and gently pushed in and out, teasing her a little more. She opened her eyes and looked up at me. As she was about to protest my teasing, I slammed hard against her. She gasped and tilted her head back. I thrust hard again and she moaned louder.

"I've wanted to do this for a long, long time, woman." I picked up speed and grabbed her hips, holding her against me. "Fuck, woman!"

"Shit, Blaine!" she gasped and let go of me. Reaching above her head, she held onto the couch. Her gaze held mine and the intensity almost knocked me backward.

I reached behind her and pulled her up. Sitting back, Penelope straddled my lap and began rotating her hips back and forth. I gripped her tits and squeezed, sucked, and licked them. Her voice reached a higher octave as I pushed up inside her.

Her hands gripped my shoulders and her moaning became louder. I watched her and, letting go of her tits, I grabbed her ass. "Fuck me, woman. Fuck me!"

"Oh God," she moaned and tilted her head back. I leaned in and flicked her pierced nipple.

"Cum for me, baby." I glanced up and watched her. Her lips parted and she inhaled sharply. I reached behind her and grabbed her hair. I yanked her head back and she groaned. "I said, cum for me."

She opened her eyes and watched me. As much as she has been pushing me away, right now, she was mine. I wanted her and she wanted me. Penelope gasped and ground her hips harder against me.

"Blaine…" my name was a whisper on her lips. The sound of it, the way she looked into my eyes… I was done for. She owned my heart.

"Penelope, I'm going to cum. Fuck… Cum baby! Cum!" I gripped her hips tighter and thrust up against her. She yelled out and clutched my shoulders tighter. I felt her nails draw blood, but I would deal with that later. She screamed out and her body went rigid. Warmth spilled inside her when I came. My body shook slightly.

I held this woman against me, never wanting to let her go. She relaxed into my embrace and rested her head on my shoulder. She kissed my neck softly and sighed.

14

*P*enelope sat on the couch beside me and pulled her knees up to her chest. She would peek over to me occasionally. Chills caressed her body and she shivered.

"Cold?" I asked her. She nodded without looking up. I rose from the couch and walked over to one of the closets in the room. Along with towels, I kept blankets.

"Just in case," I had told Chuck one day. *"Never know when they'll be of use."* I knew what they had been used for. The occasional fuck fest in the recording room and nights I would go on a drinking binge. I would lock myself in the room and drink into oblivion. Chuck knew this but never held it against me.

I pulled out a dark blue blanket made of soft cotton. Unfolding it, I walked back over to Penelope and wrapped it around her body. She glanced up at me then quickly averted her gaze. I wasn't sure if she was embarrassed being naked, or if she was starting to regret having sex.

"Are you okay?" I asked her.

She nodded then sighed. "You wanted me to sing that song, right?" I nodded and continued to watch her. She stood and allowed the blanket to cover her body. I wasn't sure what to make of her mood change, but decided to go with it.

I went over to where my shorts and boxer briefs laid and pulled them back on. I grabbed my t-shirt and pulled it over my head. Picking up her clothes I walked them over to her. She took them and sat them on the couch.

Penelope made her way over to one of the open mics and sat on a stool beside it. She adjusted the mic until it was in front of her and spoke into it.

"Test?"

"I, umm, need to turn it on first." I grinned at her. She smiled and blushed slightly.

"I knew that."

"Right." I winked. "Alright, here are the words. Read them over and think of how you'd like to sing it. I wrote it in the chord of C." I handed over my notes and she skimmed it. Penelope closed her eyes and inhaled deeply, then slowly, let it go.

"Can you give me a moment?" She glanced up and for a moment, she looked sad.

I studied her face and my heart began to hurt in my chest. I'm not sure what was going on between us, but I wanted to yell to the world that I loved this woman and that she was mine. However, if I did, I'm concerned she'd run off screaming. "Yeah, I'll be in the other room."

I lowered my gaze and walked out of the room. When I closed the studio door behind me, I glanced back through the window and found her watching me. She looked like someone had just told her that a car had hit her dog. Hell, I wanted to go back in there and hold her, tell her everything would be alright... and tell her I loved her.

Then she broke eye contact. She glanced at the words in front of her and sighed. I turned away from the door and made my way to the control center. I took a seat and turned on her mic.

After turning on a few control boards, I listened in on her

whispering the words to herself. She was becoming the musician, Penny Wise, not the person, Penelope. Her game face was on and she looked in control.

I leaned into my mic and spoke. "I'm ready when you are." She looked up through the glass and nodded.

"I'm ready." Penny glanced back down to her music and twisted her neck a few times. She sat up straight then rolled her shoulders. "Yes, ready."

Nodding, I pressed the record button. Then the magic began. She opened her mouth and pure beauty came out in the form of our song.

Here I am
Another night
Standing outside your door
I need my fix
The one only you can give me
I need you to wrap your arms around me
Calm my fears
Dry my tears

Bring me back from the brink
Hold me through the dark of night
Lay down beside me
And heal me with your touch

The pain consumes me
Demons dance around me
Laughing and jousting me to fall into their plight
Down on my knees I fall
My head hung down as the tears fall

Bring me back from the brink
Hold me through the dark of night

Lay down beside me
And heal me with your touch

You save me from the dark
Slay away all the pains
Quench my needs fulfill my wants
Heal me with just one touch
Give me the hope that someday
I will be whole again
No longer will I be hanging of the edge

Bring me back from the brink
Hold me through the dark of night
Lay down beside me
And heal me with your touch

Baby, fix me in only the way you can
Breathe life back into me
Hand in hand at the dawn of each day
We will emerge as one back from the brink

Bring me back from the brink
Hold me through the dark of night
Lay down beside me
And heal me with your touch

She stopped and her head lowered. Penny pushed the mic away and Penelope emerged. I pressed stop on recording and simply stared at the woman in the recording room. Raw emotions flooded the room and the words pierced directly into my soul.

I couldn't move; I couldn't speak. Something organic had just been created between us. This wasn't just sex, this wasn't lust; this was pure love. I knew it and Penelope knew it. What bothered me the most, though, was wondering if she was as scared as I was.

A tear slipped from her eyes and I found myself at the studio door, opening it. She glanced up at me and her bottom lip trembled. Closing the distance, I pulled her close.

"Shh, it's okay." I held onto her while she sobbed into my chest.

~

I'm not sure how much time had passed. Eventually, Penelope stopped crying and pulled away. She wiped at her face then rose from the stool to get dressed.

"The others will be here soon, I think," she started. "They'll need to fill in the music and such, right?" She glanced back at me.

"Oh, sure. I imagine Derek will be stoked to play rhythm for this. I think hearing it raw like this would…"

She cut me off. "Blaine, let's not do this."

My heart suddenly slammed against my chest. "Do what, exactly?" I stepped closer to her. Penelope shook her head no.

"This. Let's not act like a huge elephant is in the room. We need to talk about what happened and where we go from here."

I blinked. It is not often I'm caught off guard by a woman, but today was definitely that day. "I'm not sure I follow."

"I don't know if I understand what exactly is happening between us." She put her bra and panties on, followed by her tank top and cut off shorts. "I don't know if this is real."

"You have got to be kidding me." Her words cut me like a hot dagger right through my heart.

She stared into my eyes for a moment then finally, looked away. "Blaine, let's not pretend here. I heard you on your call. I heard you talking to whoever this Lexi is."

"You did? I don't appreciate being eavesdropped on."

"Consider it an investigation on my part." She stood her

ground and rested her hands on her hips. "I don't know how serious you are here. You have a reputation of being a fuck and run. I was…" she lowered her gaze, "I was vulnerable earlier. You were, too." She looked up at me again. "I don't want you to be a rebound for me. I definitely don't want to be a notch on your belt."

"You honestly think that is what this was for me? That you were just a conquest so I could… fuck you?" I felt my temper rising and I didn't want to hold back. "I fucking care for you, Penelope. Hell, I'm falling in love with you. Do you not see that?"

"Blaine, don't…"

"No, Penelope, you don't. I have wanted you for a long time. I found myself always thinking about you. Things began reminding me of you, and I wondered, if you thought of me as much. I honestly thought you did, at least your actions did."

"Would you stop for a moment before you make this into a damn fight?" She threw her arms in the air and stared at me. "Seriously, for one damn minute, stop talking!"

"Fine!"

She stared at me and shook her head. "I've been single for a short period of time. I need to know I can do this without you. I need to know that what we have… what this is between us is real. I can't do that if I'm with you twenty four seven."

"What are you saying?" Penelope closed her eyes and shook her head. "Dammit, talk. What are you trying to say?"

She sighed and looked to me again. "I'm saying that I need time to myself to know if this is real. When I come back, we'll know for sure."

"So then, what was that earlier in here? Was that a test to see if I'm good?" I shook my head and turned my back on her. I pinched the bridge of my nose. Now, I knew what Lexi felt. What all the women felt. I feel like I've been used. In the past, I would have welcomed it. Now? I don't want her to leave. I closed my eyes tightly to prevent any evidence of tears to give me away.

"It wasn't a test. We made love and it was beautiful." I felt her walk up behind me. She touched my shoulder and leaned into me. "Please, I need to do this. Not just for me, but for us. If we're really going to give this a go, I need to do this."

I turned to face her. Her eyes were filled with fear and possibly regret. I prayed it wasn't regret for sleeping with me. "This goes against everything inside me right now; I want to fight for you to stay."

"I know. But I need to do this. I don't…" she sighed and lowered her gaze. "I don't want you to be my rebound and I don't want to be your next addiction."

My eyes widened. I had not considered this, and honestly, it hurt. It hurt a lot. I had nothing else to say at this point. As much as I wanted her to stay, right now I wanted her out of my house.

I turned away from her and left the room. I unlocked the studio door and left it open. I heard Penelope sob downstairs but at that point, I didn't care. I loved this woman and she had done nothing but throw it in my face.

After making my way up the stairs to my bedroom, I closed the door and leaned against it. I closed my eyes. Her words, *I don't want you to be my rebound and I don't want to be your next addiction*, played over and over in my head. I squeezed my eyes closed and a tear managed to escape.

A moment later, I heard my front door close. Penelope was gone and I had no idea if she would ever come back. Penny Wise might return because she was under contract. But my Penelope… she could be lost to me forever.

15

*I*t has been a long, long time since I'd cried over anyone. I hadn't cried over Lexi, although I probably should have. I didn't cry when Penelope walked out my door. I did cry, though, when I realized she wasn't coming back. Two weeks have passed since I last saw her. I stared at my phone, stared at the unanswered text messages, and ignored phone calls.

"Dude, she'll be back," Derek told me. "She just needed a break from all this. From you. Hell, from life. Give her time."

"What the fuck do you think I'm doing?" I glared at him then crossed the den. I stared out the window at my front yard. A water fountain, dream cars, perfect yard... all of it material possessions. None of it meant anything to me. All I wanted was her.

"Maybe it's time everyone took a break for a while. We can't continue recording without Penny here," Matt offered in a lowered voice. I felt his hand on my shoulder. "C'mon man, let's go to the arcade or book store or something."

"No." I didn't turn to him or move.

"No? Hell, Blaine, you gotta do something."

"I don't have to do shit, alright?" I turned to glare at my best friend. "She told me she doesn't want to be my next addiction. How fucked up is that? What the fuck am I supposed to do with that?"

"Prove to her she's not an addiction," Derek offered. Matt stared at me and didn't say anything. Over the course of the years, Matt had learned that sometimes saying nothing is the best answer anyone can give.

"What?" I asked Derek.

"You heard me. Prove to her she's not…"

I cut him off. "I heard what you said. What the fuck do you mean?"

He sighed and relaxed into the couch, then crossed his ankle over his knee. "Find a way to prove to her that you love her and that she's not an addiction. How do you prove drugs are no longer an issue for you?"

"Drugs are always an issue for me. If they're in front of me, I want them. I want to use. It takes everything I have to walk away." I turned back toward the window and bit my tongue. I didn't want to continue talking about this, especially about drug use. Matt picked up on my frustration.

"Dude, enough," he told Derek. "Let it go."

The den was silent for a moment, at least until Derek had enough of the silent treatment. "Fuck this, I'm going home. Call me when we start recording again. Later." He rose from the couch and I looked over my shoulder as he walked out of the room.

"About fucking time," Matt mumbled.

"I gave them a free pass to leave over a week ago. I think he was hoping something would happen." I glanced over to Matt. "Dude, I feel like I fucked up and have no idea what I did wrong or how to fix it."

"There's nothing to do but wait. Leave her be. One way or the other, she'll be back. Unless she wants out of the band, she has no choice."

"I get that," I told Matt, "but I want her back because she

WANTS to be here, not because she has to be. Fuck I need a drink." My fingers intertwined behind my neck. "I need a hit. I need something to get me out of this funk."

"Seriously? You want a hit? You fuck."

"What did you say?" I asked Matt. My friend furrowed his brows and gave me a cold, hard stare. It scared the shit out of me when he looked this way, but I knew he always had my back, no matter what. However, right now? I think he'd rather kick it, than protect it.

"After the rehab and everything you've done, you'd drop it," he snapped his fingers, "like that, because some bitch doesn't find you worthy?"

I sighed, "She's not a bitch, asshole."

"The fuck she is! She told you she didn't want to be an addiction and didn't want you to be her rebound. Or did you only hear the first part? Because her leaving so you won't be her rebound? That right there, took balls on her part. You need to remember that and keep your own in check, fucker."

"Fuck you." I turned away from him and walked out of the den. At least until there was a shove to my back. "What the fuck, man? Did you seriously just push me?"

"I sure as hell did! What, are you going to get upset and tell me you want to use because I pushed you? Oh tell you what, I'll get a tissue and we'll sit down and cry about it. Does that sound better?" He threw his arms in the air and shook his head. "Who the fuck ARE you anymore? You mope; you're all depressed and shit. I don't fucking know you, man."

From the put down to the shove, Matt has pushed the limits on what I'm calling friendship. I closed my eyes and counted to ten, not wanting to see red when I opened them. I took in a deep breath and stood there. Matt's words went through me, but never penetrated me. He's a good guy, was there for me when I fucked up the most. "I don't understand why you're doing this."

"Why I'm doing what? Reminding you that you're Blaine? Wake the fuck up, man! She's a chick!"

I had enough. "She's MY chick! She's MINE! Do you not understand that?" I stepped closer to Matt until I was in his face. "I fucking LOVE that woman! We had sex before she left! She fucking USED me, dammit!" I pointed to myself and felt the rage peaking inside me. "I use chicks, not the other way around! I fuck'em and leave'em, not her! ME! It's me, it's always been me! Fuck, why can't you see that? I fucking LOVE her and she walked the fuck OUT on me!" There was no hiding anything now. Tears sprang from my eyes and I yelled to the top of my lungs. "FUCK!"

Matt nodded a few times then laid his hands on my shoulders. "Okay, so feel better now? How long were you going to hold that shit inside?" He grinned at me.

"Fuck you, asshole."

"There is no way you're addicted to her. I see it. Hell, Derek saw it. She'll see it when she returns, but you HAVE to give her this space, man. She's hurting, too. Remember, she broke up with her dude, most likely because of you. Do you think she really wants to carry that shit around on her shoulders? I imagine she wants to prove him wrong. I imagine she feels for you exactly how you feel for her. Let her come back and dammit, clean the fuck up. Go shower or something. When you're done, I'm taking you to the shooting range. We'll go shoot skeet and practice for the zombie apocalypse."

I couldn't help it; I chuckled. Matt had this thing about the end of the world and zombies attacking. He wanted to be prepared and honestly, with some convincing, I might let him be team leader, if this were to ever happen.

"Alright, I'm in. While we're out, I want to get new ink."

"Whatever, let's get going. I'll let Chuck know what's going on and make sure Derek has a way back."

I nodded and headed upstairs to my room. Matt was like a brother to me. He's the only one who could call me on my shit and set me straight. As much as I wanted to use, to drink… to do anything, he was there. He was my voice of reason, when mine would shut down. Between him and Chuck, they had saved me from snorting myself into oblivion.

~

We ended up at the tattoo shop longer than expected. I had a new design in mind of music notes and words from the song I wrote for Penelope to be tattooed across my side. My skin along my ribs was now red, but the pain provided a reminder I was here… and sober. I've heard that some turn their addiction to tattooing. I couldn't imagine doing this; my body would be a complete canvas and nothing would be left… especially after my blow up today.

I handed over the scribble of words to Freddie, my go-to artist.

"Bring me back from the brink. This is what you want?" Freddie asked me as he began drawing out the letters on trace paper.

"Yeah. From a song I wrote." I glanced up to Matt who in turn smiled, then nodded.

"Cool. How's this?" Freddie held up the trace paper with the words in a hard, metal type of lettering.

"Add on a few barb wires to the lettering and it would be sick."

"Got it." Freddie added on a few and showed me. I nodded and lay back down. The sound of the needle started up. I've been through this so many times, you'd think when the needle hit my skin I would be prepared. Hell no, each time the shit makes me flinch. Matt chuckled.

"Fuck you," I told him. He grinned and crossed his arms over his chest.

"Feeling better?" he asked me.

"I suppose. This does help." Freddie cleared his throat. "What?" I asked. "Out with it."

"I've come to find in my line of work, people tend to get tattoos under duress, as a way to retaliate and sometimes, boredom. Whose heart did you break?"

"Freddie, it's not like that," I told him. "There's this chick, Penny Wise."

"Dude, like the fucking clown? Damn, that's sick!" Freddie chuckled and continued the art work.

"Yeah, we thought so, too. Anyway, we started seeing each other and shit started getting real. She…" I trailed off and sighed.

"She had to return home to figure a few things out on her own," Matt finished for me. I glanced up at him and he nodded. I lowered my gaze to the floor and stared at the tile.

"You love her?" Freddie asked me.

"What?" I think my breath may have caught in my throat.

"You heard me, man. Do you love the chick?" He wiped a napkin over my skin and continued.

"I think so, yeah, pretty sure I do."

"Pretty sure and you think so isn't *fuck yes I love this woman*. If you love her, you tell her. Don't say shit unless you mean it. Chicks hate that. If you love her, and I mean, you'd lay down your life for her, love her, then tell her and get it out there. Don't do it in an open area where she can't freak out. Because trust me, bitches like to show off and shit." He chuckled, wiped my skin, and continued the tattoo. "All I'm saying is tell her how you feel. If she left to, as your buddy said, sort shit out, she just needs to know you're in it for her, not for yourself."

I thought about this for a moment. I knew he was right. Hell, Matt was right about this also. "When did you become all Doctor Feelgood?" I grinned.

Freddie wiped my skin one last time and examined his work. "Alright dude, you're done. Check it out. Let me know if you need anything touched up."

I rose from the tattoo bench and walked across the room. Lifting my arm, I examined the art work. My body had changed so much since I'd left Texas. Once a smaller, thinner build, now my arms and chest were thick with muscle. My skin has tattoos over most of it. My eyes... damn, my eyes look tired. Being clean definitely has its advantages in seeing life for what it is, not what you think it should be.

"Looks fucking awesome, man. Thanks." I walked back and Freddie applied ointment and a wrap to my skin.

"Anytime. You up, Matt?"

"Fuck no. I'm a pussy when it comes to needles."

Freddie chuckled and I shook my head. I paid the man and we took off.

Shooting skeet seemed to be far from Matt's mind now, and honestly, I'm okay with that. Considering the shit I stirred while using, it wouldn't be much fun for me anyway. I wasn't a big fan of guns. Guns were Matt's hobby, whereas mine was music.

A little while later, we pulled into the garage and parked. My side hurt but it would heal in time. I needed to clean it some, then head down to the studio. I needed the distraction music would provide. I had the itch to write another song; maybe something for Deep Ember. They've been through hell and back with me.

"I'm gonna take off. Got shit to do." Matt waved as he walked out the garage door. I waited until he had started up his car before I shut the garage door. I remember my mother doing that with her friends when they would visit.

"It's the right thing to do, Blaine," my mother would say. "We need to make sure they take off and have no car trouble."

As the garage door began to lower, I walked inside and closed the door behind me. When I turned and walked into the den, nothing could have prepared me for what was waiting inside.

16

*P*enelope rose from the couch and stared at me. She looked scared... almost fearful. Her hair was pulled around her shoulder and she had on a tight fitting sundress. She looked beautiful. I blinked and hoped... no prayed I wasn't dreaming.

"Penelope?" I took a few steps forward and she lowered her gaze. Folding her hands in front of her, she shifted her weight on her feet.

"Hi, Blaine." Her voice was soft... tender. She raised her eyes and watched me for a moment. "Your staff allowed me in. I hope that's okay?"

"Of course it is. When did you get back?" I wanted to run to her, tell her I loved her, and tell her I'd only thought of her. Something else decided to hold off... the voice in my head. *Don't, let her speak*, it told me.

"I need to tell you a few things. I need you to let me get it out, before you say anything." I nodded and raised my brows. "While I was gone, I was miserable. I cried, no... scratch that. I fucking sobbed." She paused for a moment while I watched her.

Penelope's features shifted from scared to upset. I had no idea what was going through her mind, or what she had been through while she was gone. I only hoped she'd continue and let me in.

"I cried so much, Blaine. I found myself missing you. I missed your presence. I missed being near you. I missed your stupid jokes. Hell, I missed just being next to you, waking up with you in bed, even joking with the bands.

"I felt like I was falling in love with you. I needed to know that I wasn't in love with the idea of someone wanting me...needing me. I needed to know we were in this for the long run, Blaine, not just a five minute romance." She paused and turned away from me. Her arms wrapped around her slender frame and she lowered her head.

I wanted to go to her, hold her, and tell her I love her, but again, I hesitated.

"Penelope..."

"I'm not done, Blaine." She looked over her shoulder at me. "There's more."

"Alright." I walked over and took a seat on the couch. I had no idea what was more, but I had a feeling it wasn't good. My heart pounded in my chest as I waited. For what? I had no idea. She held my heart in her hands and she was the only one who could continue holding it... or she could be the one to break it.

"My life growing up wasn't fun. You know more about me than my ex ever did. With him, he seemed to love and care about me. Well, at least I thought he did." She shrugged slightly then turned to face me. "I need someone that will support me, guide me, and be my rock when I need them. I need a partner in life, a lover, and a best friend. I need someone who will be all in."

She paused for a long moment and just stared at me. I'm afraid to blink, fearing if I do, this moment will pass. I want to tell her I will be all these things for her. I want to make love to her every fucking day of my damn life. Hell, I would be willing to put a damn ring on her finger if that's what it took to prove it.

However, I can't help but feel with all that she has said, there will be a "but" following shortly.

"But?" I finally asked and broke the tension between us.

She furrowed her brows and stood a little straighter. "I didn't say but."

"But you will."

"No, there's no but. This is me, putting it out there for you, what I want and need. This is me telling you I'm in."

I don't say anything; hell, I can't. I'm speechless and honestly, this is a first. My lips part and I'm caught off guard at her confession. Penelope is here… telling me she wants me… no one else, just me.

"Blaine," she pleaded, "say something!"

"Shit, baby, I'm sorry." I stood and quickly closed the distance between us. I pulled her close to me and hugged her tightly. Her body fit against mine as if she were made for me.

I inhaled and breathed in her strawberry scent. My eyes closed and I smiled. Her arms wrapped around my body and I suddenly flinched.

"Oh, did I hurt you?" She stepped back and stared at me with a concerned look on her face.

I chuckled. "No, but I did get ink done today."

"Oh," she grinned.

I reached for her and touched her cheek. She leaned into my palm and closed her eyes. She was absolutely stunning and she was mine.

"I love you, Penelope."

She opened her eyes and smiled. "I love you, too, Blaine."

"So… you wanna go steady?" I waggled my brows and she giggled. She nodded a few times. "Excellent." I stepped closer and cupped her cheeks. I leaned in and kissed her.

Her hands moved up my biceps while I deepened the kiss, trailing my tongue along her lips. She was here and she was now mine. My heart was beating rapidly. I ended the kiss a little too soon and pressed my forehead to hers. "There's something I need to tell you as well."

"Oh, okay." She swiped her finger along my lower lip. I smiled and brushed her hair behind her ear.

"The night we made out when you had too much to drink?" She nodded and I continued. "In the past, I would have been just as wasted and would have had no issue taking advantage of the situation. But that night, I was sober and saw things very clearly. It was that night that I realized how much I wanted you, no needed you in my life. I wanted you so badly, Penelope. Fuck, you had me so hard." I shook my head recalling the night in my bedroom.

Penelope pressed her palms against my chest and leaned into me. The grin on her lips was mischievous and I knew she was contemplating something. Good god, she turned me on with this simple look.

"Well, I'm completely sober now and very much awake." She moved her hands around my neck and pulled me closer. She kissed my cheek and whispered in my ear, "What are you going to do about that?" She flicked her tongue against my earlobe, causing me to groan.

My hands were lying on her hips and I moved them around to her ass. I squeezed it and pulled her closer to me. My nose grazed hers and her lips parted. "I plan on taking you up to my room, having my way with you for a few hours, and probably again tonight. Oh, there might be shower sex involved."

She shivered in my grasp and I knew she wanted this as much as I did. I could see the longing in her eyes. I continued to look into her sky blue eyes until she had enough and claimed my lips. Her arms tightened around my neck and I lifted her, her legs wrapping around my waist.

After I carried her upstairs to my room, stumbling once on the stairs and our laughter carrying throughout the house, we finally made it to my bedroom. I kicked the door closed and pressed her back against it. I fumbled with the lock until it finally latched.

My hands moved to her breasts and I kneaded them as we continued to kiss. She bit my lip and licked my tongue in a seductive way that caused my dick to throb.

"Fuck, woman," I whispered. I carried her to my bed and we collapsed on top of it. I kissed down to her neck while her fingers tugged at the material of my shirt.

"Shit, watch the tat, woman."

"I'm sorry! Are you okay?" She bit her lip when I looked at her. I grinned.

"Hell yeah, I'm fine. Now come here." I kissed her again and she tugged at my hair.

"Get naked," she ordered. Who was I to disappoint? She sat up and pulled her dress over her head. She reached back and unfastened her red, see-through bra, then slowly removed it. She tossed it and slapped my hands as I went to grab her breasts.

"What the fuck, woman?" I asked. Penelope grinned and massaged her breasts for me. She pinched the nipples and pulled them. "Oh fuck." The words came out of my mouth and she laughed.

"Come here." She reached for me and pulled me close. I kissed her and pushed her back onto the bed. I massaged her breasts and slowly kissed my way down to her neck. I nibbled on her skin as she gasped.

"You're so beautiful," I whispered. Her hands moved up my biceps and would occasionally grip harder as I nibbled against her flesh. I moved farther down and looked upon her taut nipples. Fuck, they were beautiful. I licked against her piercing and she gasped. The nipple automatically responded to me and became erect. I glanced to the other and pinched it.

"Blaine, fuck!"

I looked up to her and she grinned. "Harder?"

She nodded.

Oh. Fuck. Yes.

I captured her nipple with my mouth and my tongue flicked her piercing. She moaned and pressed herself harder against me. I released her nipple then captured the other one. Her hands moved into my hair and she held me close. Hell, I needed more.

I released her breast and began moving down her body. I kissed along her flat stomach until I reached her panties. The ones she had on matched her bra and like it, they were see-through.

I felt my mouth salivate. I glanced back at her and found her biting her lip. Oh, she wanted this as much as I did. I grinned and leaned down, kissing the inside of her thighs. Gently, my nose grazed across the lining of her panties. She was wet and I wanted to taste her.

My fingers hooked into either side of her panties and I pulled them down her legs. Fuck me; she was hot! I pushed her legs apart and paused. I looked at her and tilted my head. "Are you ready for this?"

She nodded and smiled. "I want you. Please."

I grinned and raised a single brow. "Good answer." She grinned and I lowered myself.

I kissed against her folds and she hissed softly. I barely touched her skin with my tongue and she whimpered.

"Blaine, don't tease!"

I grinned then separated her folds with my tongue, feeling her clit. She moaned softly into the air. I did it again, and this time, I sucked it into my mouth, thrashing it with my tongue.

Her hips bucked against me. I held her close and licked her pussy as she moaned. She grabbed my hair again and began to grind against my mouth. I could taste her honey; I could taste her arousal. I wanted to taste her when she came.

I inserted a finger inside her and she moaned again. I pressed against the G spot and massaged it. Penelope almost came unglued in my grasp. She moaned louder and I flicked harder against her clit. I inserted another finger and she arched her back.

"Fuck, Blaine!" When she yelled my name, I growled against her pussy. She moaned louder and I felt her body shudder. Penelope came hard and fast.

I pulled away and watched her for a moment, smiling. I wiped my face off and began unbuttoning my pants. Her chest rose and fell from the aftershocks of her orgasm.

"Are you okay?" I asked her.

She smiled and nodded a few times. "Fuck, yes!" She laughed to herself. I stood off the bed and kicked off my shoes, then removed my pants and boxer briefs. She looked over and raised a brow, then looked at me. "I didn't get a real good look at you the day in the bathroom then in the studio… well it all happened so fast. You're… umm… Blaine, you're huge!"

I chuckled and looked down at my cock, then back at her. "You took it fine the other day. Now sit back and let me have you, sexy." I climbed onto the bed and hovered just above her. She opened her legs for me and my cock rubbed against her slick folds.

"Blaine," she whispered my name. I leaned in and kissed her. Penelope sighed into my mouth. "Make love to me."

I kissed her harder and reached down between us. Pressing my head against her entrance, I pushed inside her.

I began moving inside her at a slow, gentle pace. I kissed her lips, then her cheek. She moved her head to the side and offered her neck. I kissed her and nibbled on her ear.

"You're so beautiful," I whispered… and she was.

"Blaine," she whispered my name and I felt her move underneath me. I pushed a little more and she responded with a moan. I pulled back and thrust into her. Her back arched and she gripped my arms.

I prayed I had not hurt her. "Shit, are you okay? Did I…"

She cut me off. "Fuck, yes! Don't stop!"

I grinned and lifted myself to my elbows. I pulled back and began thrusting inside her. Her body moved with mine and she was stunning. She opened her eyes and looked up, watching me.

She grinned and held onto my biceps. I pulled back and thrust hard inside her. Penelope gasped, then moaned. Her arms reached above her head and she grasped the headboard.

I sat back and grabbed her hips, then pulled her closer to me. Holding her hips in the air, I moved hard against her. I gritted my teeth and watched her breasts move with her body. Fuck, she was beautiful.

Penelope moaned with each thrust, occasionally yelling my name. I felt the orgasm building and I slowed down. She looked up at me with a curious gaze. I sat her body back on the bed and reached for her breasts, massaging them.

"I'm about to cum," I told her.

She grinned. "Is that so?" She sat up and grabbed a hold of my shoulders. She pulled herself up and began grinding. My arms wrapped around her as I held her close.

"Fuck woman, I'm going to cum if you don't stop!"

She grinned and stopped moving. She lay back on the bed and her arms moved above her head. I watched her and my eyes roamed over her body. Slowly, I began moving against her. I knew that no matter what, whether we made love fast or slow, I was about to cum, one way or the other.

"Fuck, I can't stop. I'm going to cum!" I grabbed her hips and began thrusting hard and fast against her. Penelope's back arched and she gripped my arms tight. "Fuck!"

"Blaine," she yelled, "holy shit!"

I lost myself inside her. I thrusted twice more, then panted. I watched her for a moment as she slowed her breathing. I pulled out and lay beside her. Catching my own breath, I gently touched her cheek then kissed her. "Are you okay?"

"Oh, I'm great," she told me with a smile. "Give me a few minutes because we're doing this again."

I chuckled and kissed her. "Good. Then come take a shower with me." I winked and moved off the bed to make my way toward the bathroom.

After I turned on the water, I looked up to find her watching me from the door entrance. She was still naked and damn, she was beautiful.

"You are the sexiest, most beautiful woman I have ever been with." I motioned for her to join me. I wrapped my arms around her and gently kissed her lips. "I love you."

"Mmm," she kissed me again. "I love you, too."

I reached in and tested the water. "It's perfect. Come on." The bathroom shower was huge. I relished my bathroom with the dual heads and body sprayers.

We stepped under the sprayers and I pulled her close. The water ran down her body and when she grazed her fingers through her hair, my dick immediately responded.

I leaned in and captured her piercing with my lips. My hands pulled her body close to mine. I kissed up her chest and captured her lips. Penelope reached between us, wrapped her fingers around my cock, and gave it a gentle squeeze.

"You tasted me, now I want to taste you." She smirked and kissed me once again.

"Fuck me; that's hot, woman." I leaned against the wall as she kissed along my chest, and slowly lowered herself. She stroked me a few times then licked the tip of my head. She glanced up at me once and smirked, then took my length inside her mouth.

I groaned and my head tilted back. She sucked my cock and it was like magic. I glanced back down and grabbed a fistful of her hair. I didn't force her any harder than what she was already doing, but I definitely pressed her onward.

"Fuck sakes, woman." I groaned and continued watching her. She cupped my balls and squeezed them. "Shit," I whispered.

She pulled off my length and glanced up. "I want you to fuck me."

Oh, hell yes. I took her hands and helped her stand. I kissed her hard and grabbed a handful of her ass, squeezing it. She gasped against my lips. I turned her around and bent her over.

Feeling her entrance, she was wet and ready. I pressed against her and shoved inside. Gripping her hips, I began to thrust. Her hands pressed against the tile wall and my body slapped hard against hers.

"Blaine! Fuck!" She moaned as I thrust harder.

"Fuck, baby!" I growled. "Fuck, you feel so good!"

She whimpered, "I'm afraid I'll be too sore to sit down."

"I'll take care of that," I grunted. "I'll rub ice on your pussy, if it'll make you feel better."

She looked over her shoulder at me with a grin. "You'd like that, wouldn't you?"

"Fuck yeah I'd like that!" I gripped a handful of her hair and pulled her head back. She moaned louder. "I'm going to fucking cum, baby!"

"Yes!" She yelled. "Yes, fuck me!"

I groaned once more, and then giving her one last thrust, I came. "Penelope!" My voice echoed through the bathroom when I yelled out her name.

She grinned and stood up once I pulled out of her. "I really will be sore later, baby." She touched my cheek and kissed me.

I wrapped my arms around her and held her close. The water continued to shower down on us and I lightly kissed her forehead. "I'm serious; I'll rub ice on it if you like." I winked and kissed her back. "Come on, let me wash you."

"ou know the bands will be back soon," I told Penelope. "Derek flew in today and Matt is on his way back with him."

She sat in my lap on the couch and pulled her legs up to her chest. She leaned into me and kissed on my neck. "Good. I've missed them." Her hand moved across my chest, to my neck then cupped my cheek. She leaned in and kissed me, then teased my lips with her tongue.

"Woman, start that up and we'll do it here on the couch."

"You're such a tease, baby." She giggled and kissed me again.

The front door opened and laughter carried inside. Matt was the first to step into the den and he stopped and stared... then blinked. He grinned and shook his head.

In followed Jordan, who chuckled. "About fucking time."

"Excuse me?" Penelope asked, as she grinned.

"No, just saying: about fucking time." Jordan grinned and came over to us, shook my hand then stepped back.

Joe stepped in next and nodded. "Cool." I chuckled.

"What's going on in..." Derek stopped mid step and mid word. He stared between me and Penelope for a moment. His brows furrowed and he closed the distance to the couch. "If you hurt her," he paused when Penelope climbed off my lap.

"Listen here. You started this shit, Derek. Let it go. He won't hurt me. He loves me. Don't you, baby?" She glanced back to me and I grinned.

"Sure do. She's the shit; I love her."

"See?" she asked and put her hands on her hips. "Now if you're done being holier than thou," she sat back in my lap and my arms went around her waist. I kissed her neck softly and she tilted her head. I wondered for a moment if she forgot what she was going to say.

Derek cleared his throat. "Got it. You two are fucking now. And in love. Yeah, go have your rock star babies and shit."

"Derek!" Penelope yelled. I couldn't help it, I laughed hard. So did Matt.

"Well, now that we're one big happy fucking family here," I started.

Derek held his hands up. "Hang on; I'm not fucking anyone here."

"What?" I asked.

Matt bent over laughing. "That's not what he meant, you idiot." He laughed again then, when he gained his composure, he motioned for Derek to continue.

"Fuck you, asshat!" Derek sat down on the couch. "If you were gay you better believe I'd be tapping that ass of yours. Watch yourself, Matt, I might sneak in your room later."

Matt suddenly sobered, and stared at Derek. "I so don't swing that way man, but I'm flattered."

Penelope giggled.

"Right, now that this has turned awkward, we have music to record. Derek," he turned his attention to me as I continued. "Penelope recorded our new song. We need your rhythm behind it." Derek nodded. "Jordan, you up to playing, maybe some keyboard in it?"

"Yeah, that's cool. I need to hear the melody and shit though."

We ventured downstairs to the studio. I took a seat in front of the studio deck and turned it on. Maneuvering through the music, I pulled up Penelope's song, *Bring Me Back From the Brink.*

"This was recorded a few weeks ago." I glanced over at her and motioned her over. I pulled her in my lap and kissed her shoulder. "It was raw and had a lot of emotion behind it. Check it out. If we need to re-record, we can set it up, but if we can, I want to keep this."

I pressed play and the room went silent, except for the sound of Penelope's voice. Her song flooded the room. Jordan closed his eyes and listened to the rhythm. Penelope turned sideways in my lap and leaned into me.

"I love you," she whispered. "I loved you, then."

"I know," I whispered back. I kissed her softly and she smiled.

The song continued to play. I glanced around the room and did a double take at Derek. He had sat on the couch and his eyes were closed; a tear streaked down his cheek. I tapped Penelope to look and she glanced over. She rose quietly from my lap and crossed the room. She sat down on her knees in front of him and took his hands in hers.

Derek opened his eyes in surprise and stared at her for a moment. He leaned forward and pulled her in a hug. They held onto one another for a few minutes, then he let her go. There was something in this song, in this moment, that moved Derek. I'm not sure if it was a memory or an experience, but either way, we would be here for him, as my band had been for me.

The song ended and the room remained silent. I looked around at everyone and no one said a word.

Penelope stood and wrung her fingers together. "Well? What did y'all think?"

"It was beautiful," Derek told her. "Perfect." She smiled at him.

"I don't think it needs keys, Blaine." Jordan announced. "I think a rhythm guitar and maybe… maybe a bass for percussion, but that's it."

I nodded in agreement. "Alright, well, let's set it up and see where we get.

I glanced over at Derek and found him watching me. He nodded once. I grinned and stood. Having Derek's approval would be up there with having her father's, in a way. I don't imagine I'll ever meet her dad, but I wish I could have met her mom.

"Well," I made my way toward the sound room and waited, "once we're done here, I need to take Penelope with me to Texas. There's people she needs to meet."

"There is?" She asked me.

"Yep. You get to meet my mother, and if time allows, the Senator of Texas."

"How the fuck do you know the Senator?" Derek asked in surprise.

"He's married to Blaine's high school sweetheart," Penelope announced.

Matt stared at her and raised a brow. He then glanced at me. "That a good idea, man?"

"Yep. They might be expecting me, soon." I announced.

"How so?" He asked, obviously confused.

"I might have called."

Matt raised his brows in surprise. "And?"

"And nothing. We talked. All three of us."

"Everything is cool," Penelope interjected.

"You were in on it?" Matt asked and rubbed his neck. "Damn, I missed a lot."

"Not exactly," she told him then shrugged. "Details don't matter. She was a big part of his life so I'd like to get to know his past. Who knows," she shrugged, "maybe we can be friends."

"Not likely," Matt offered.

"Why not?" Penelope asked.

"From what I remember of this Lexi girl, she kicked the ass of last the bitch that fucked with Blaine."

She laughed. "She has no reason to touch me. Besides," Penelope walked over and slid her arms around my waist. "Blaine is mine, not hers."

"That's right, baby." I kissed her softly and grinned.

"That's it. I need to get laid," Matt announced.

"Want to join us for a threesome?" Penelope offered.

"What?" Matt and I asked at the same time.

She laughed and shook her head. "I'm confident enough in my relationship with you to share you with another man, lover." She pursed her lips to keep from giggling then miserably failed.

"You know that shit is not happening anywhere near my ass."

"Dude!" Derek yelled. "Seriously?"

"No offense, man," I offered. Matt chuckled and Penelope giggled.

"You are mine, Blaine. I am not sharing you with anyone."

EPILOGUE

*I*t's hard to believe two years have passed since I met Penelope. She's become my world, my reason for living a somewhat normal life…my everything. Mongrels of Soul have since gone platinum. Some thought I couldn't do it, couldn't think of someone other than myself. Hell, I used to think the same thing. I always came first. My drug habit, my sense of self and no one else. Now? Well, now I come first in taking care of myself. I have been clean going on four years and they're the best years of my life so far.

Penelope comes next. I love this woman, heart and soul. The relationship I have with her is nothing like I've ever experienced. I had a closeness with Lexi. She knew me as I once was, before the drugs. Some people come into your life for a reason. Penelope's reason was to keep me level headed and clean. This I was sure of. Without her patience, without her in my life, I'm positive I would have eventually fallen off the deep end. I would have found myself in a drug-induced coma or I would have died.

She told me once she did not want to be my next addiction. Well, if loving someone is an addiction, then sign me up. I couldn't get enough of this woman.

Penelope would slap her bass like no one else. She could scream into the microphone and make it sound like love. She could capture and control her audience, with hardly a blink.

"Blaine?" Her voice pulled me from my thoughts. I smiled as I glanced over at her. She had her hair curled in ringlets and had a new pattern of stars etched into the side of her shaved head. She went as far as dying a few patches of stars red. Her too tight tank top with Mongrels of Soul written across the front hugged itself around her breasts. The plaid school girl skirt paired with a pair of white knee highs made my cock jump to attention. She played the innocent look very well. Her black Mary Jane's had rhinestone encrusted skulls on the tops of them.

As my eyes made their way back up her slender frame, the glint of her diamond caught my attention. I asked Penelope to marry me during the holidays. She said yes. Tonight we were celebrating our engagement, as well as our love song making the top ten chart five weeks in a row. *Back From the Brink* had gone platinum. We recorded a music video and it debuted today on *MTV*. Penelope didn't say a word about it during the final taping and play back. Today was another story. Today, when she saw it on TV, the woman squealed, jumped up and down, and then hugged me tight.

"Are you ready to greet your most trusted fans?" I asked her with a smile. Closing the distance, I pulled her next to me. Vanilla infused lotion filled my senses. I kissed her cheek and squeezed her ass. "Damn, are you not wearing panties?" I pulled back with a smirk and saw the look of mischief in her eyes.

"Nope," she grinned then kissed me softly on the lips. "I wanted to take a moment to thank you for all of this."

I shook my head with a smile. "There's nothing to thank me for. You and Mongrels did all of this. I simply recorded the process."

"No, it's not that. You saw something in us immediately. You said you saw greatness in us. It took some convincing on

Derek's part, but I think the realization he's a mega star has finally sunk in. That, and maybe the Corvette he recently bought."

I chuckled. "The car is sick. And anyone who did not see the talent in your band is a damned fool. Besides," I kissed her softly, "I get to take one of the members home with me each night and make love to her." I winked and kissed her again.

"Who, Derek?" She giggled.

"You really went there?" I shook my head. "I'll show you how into you I am." I waggled my brows.

"I don't think we have enough time to have sex, baby. We go on in ten minutes."

"Nah, that's more than enough time. I need like three, tops." I grinned and she laughed.

"Well, then, what are we waiting for?" Penelope turned and walked across the room, putting a little sway in her step. She stopped in front of a desk inside the green room and bent over. The woman was definitely not wearing panties. Fuck me; she was slit to ass, right in front of me. She peeked over her shoulder and made a 'come here' motion with her finger.

I licked my lips and closed the distance. Shit, I love this woman. My cock was already at attention and I rubbed it against the jeans I was wearing. I unbuttoned my pants, and pushed them and my boxers down to my ankles. Lining up to her, I pushed in and grabbed her hips.

Penelope gasped and grabbed hold of the desk. "You realize," she started and moaned softly, "Anyone could walk in and catch us."

"Good, more exciting and more reason to fuck you hard and quick." I grabbed her hips tight and thrust against her. Her moans grew louder. "Fuck, baby!"

"Yes," she gasped between moans. "Fuck me!"

It was maybe two minutes and I came. "I am so fucking you again later tonight."

"You better," she said as she stood up straight. "I'll be right back." She kissed me softly then turned to go to the bathroom.

The door to the green room opened and Matt stuck his head inside. He raised a brow and stared at me. "Well, I see I have good timing." He chuckled and stepped in. "You walk with your pants down much?"

I looked down, then back at my best friend. "What can I say? I'm starting a fashion trend." I reached down and pulled my clothes up. "The band ready?"

"Fucking house is full, man. I know we said family and some friends, but I didn't realize they had this many friends."

"Dude, you know how it is. Friends know friends. Everyone wants in."

"Fortunately, House of Blues can support it," Matt said and leaned against the desk.

I raised a brow and glanced down with a smirk. "I wouldn't come any closer."

Matt glanced down and flinched. "Is that…" He glanced at me then back down.

"Yep." I chuckled at the repulsed look on Matt's face. "Dude, when you get off, you know we have no control of where it might land."

He shook his head. "That's fucked up, man. Warn a dude."

Penelope walked out of the bathroom and smiled. "Any sooner and we'd have had a threesome." She winked at us. I knew she was teasing but Matt didn't. If looks could speak alone, there's telling what he'd say. His mouth was as wide as his eyes.

"Dude, she's kidding. Tell him you're kidding," I said with a grin.

"Oh yeah, I'm kidding. I mean, it's not every day a girl can claim to be sleeping with two members of Deep Ember. Imagine that headline."

I chuckled. "Get over here, sexy." I pulled her into my arms and kissed her.

"Umm..." Matt was still at a loss for words. He looked at the door and pushed off the desk. "I'll, umm," he pointed to the door and walked toward it. "Yeah, see you out there." He closed the door behind him.

Penelope laughed. "He's too easy. I have panties on now. But later, shred them, baby!"

I chuckled. "Are you ready for this? Your fans await, Penny Wise." She nodded. "Then go get'em, superstar."

She grinned and quickly struck the famous pose coined by the comedian from Saturday Night Live. She lunged and threw her arms in the air and yelled, "Superstar!"

I shook my head. "Get out there, Penny. See you backstage." I kissed her and, as she turned away, I watched the love of my life walk through the green room door, onto the stage that had completely changed our lives.

THE END
Continue the series with the next book in the Southern Roots series, Fueled Desire!
Here's chapter one!

*S*eeing Lexi on the television next to her Senator husband was too much for me. That should have been me up there on his arm... the Senator's wife, not her. The farmer's daughter life is what Lexi had. I grew up with wealth and a damn silver spoon. What do I have to show for it? Nothing. Does anyone care? Hardly.

Every fucking day Mama makes a point to tell me how disappointed she is in me. Some days I wonder if she is actually talking about me... or possibly herself.

She's been drunk almost every night since I was about twelve.

If my father had not made the investments he did and made the money that soon came after, I often wonder if he would have been home more. I wonder if this would have made a difference with Mama, or even our relationship.

I sighed and lay back on my bed. I stared at my ceiling for a while as thoughts ran through my mind.

Traveling the world.

Scotland.

India.

Australia.

All the different places I have always wanted to see, but never took the time. I've been so busy with my own life, trying to please Mama, trying to be the good daughter, that I never took any time for me. The real me; the me that was trapped inside, dying to get out. It never changed.

Hell, even when I was fucking Blaine behind Lexi's back, I never considered how this would make her feel. Blaine was mine. Well, at least in my mind he was… until the night he demanded I tell Robert he was fucking Lexi in the bathroom and not me. That moment clarified exactly what I was doing.

I closed my eyes and a tear slipped into my hair. As I wiped it off, the words slut, tramp, and whore ran through my mind. I often heard these from Mama and I sometimes heard people whisper it behind my back. I always thought they were jealous…

Well, no more will I be slut, tramp, and whore. As of today, as of right now, I'm the new Abby Masters. I refuse to be anything else. I refuse to be used and abused any longer.

Oh, poor little rich girl. I snorted at the thought. "Yeah, fuck you society and what you think of me." I flipped off the then sat up. I had enough money saved that I could back pack across Europe if I wanted. Then again, my version of back packing is staying in a Hilton. I shook my head and made my way into my closet.

The light flicked on as I walked inside. My clothes from different designers, some of them worn once, some with price tags still on them, stared at me. I touched a few of the garments and wondered why I had wanted these so badly when I bought them.

"Probably because someone else eyed them. Heaven forbid someone have something I don't." Where the hell did I go wrong? When did I become this person? I sighed and shoved at my designer tops. A suitcase sat in wait in the back of my closet. If it had been a beacon, it would have lit up. I grabbed it and opened it up. I could relate to the emptiness inside. No contents… like my heart.

"Fuck this shit. I'm changing and I'm outta this fuckhole town."

⁓

"What do you mean you're leaving?" Mama was slightly buzzed. It was two in the afternoon. I think I was a little disappointed, she's usually three sheets to the wind by now.

"Just what I said, Mama. I'm leaving. I want to explore the world and I can't do it living here."

She laughed and shook her head. "What, honey, did you fuck all the men in town and need fresh meat?"

To say I was shocked at her words doesn't begin to cover how I felt. She's my mother, yet, for some reason, she absolutely hates me.

"Oh don't be so shocked, child." She patted my face with a smirk. "I'm sure you'll have some idiot under your spell very soon. That's one asset your father gave you." She snorted and turned her back to me.

I had half a mind to throw something at her. The vase in the den was looking pretty good. "Well, I can see I'll be missed here," I said to her sarcastically. I squeezed my eyes to keep the tears from giving me away. I would not give her the satisfaction of crying. She had taken too many tears from me already. "Good bye, Mama.

I'll tell Daddy I left. Coming from you, you might make it sound like you forced me to leave."

"Whatever," she mumbled, then she tripped. The wall caught her fall and she left an indention in the molding. Maybe she's a little more drunk than I thought. "Good God, child, get the fuck out of my house before you force me to kick your ass out!" Her voice rose in a scream.

I quickly turned away and left the den. My hands were wiping my cheeks as I made my way to the front door. My suitcase was packed with a few days' worth of clothes. Anything else I would need, I would pick it up on the way.

Good thing Daddy put my car in my name. Mama would probably call the police and tell them that it was stolen.

As I made my way outside and closed the door behind me, I suddenly couldn't breathe. I sucked in air but it wasn't making its way into my lungs. I felt like I was drowning. I coughed hard and bent over, then caught myself on my suitcase.

"Ms. Abby, are you okay, Ms. Abby?" Scott, our gardener was suddenly at my side. His hand touched my back and he bent over to look at my face.

I turned and glanced in his direction and at his words, are you okay, I realized... I was. I nodded a few times then finally, took in a deep breath.

"Yes, Scott, thank you. For once, I think I'm okay. No wait, I know I'm okay." I smiled and wondered if I were having some kind of panic attack. I've never been on my own, aside from my dorm in college. Not that *that* counts, of course.

"May I get you some water, Ms. Abby?" Scott was a nice man. My family didn't deserve someone nice. They didn't deserve much of anything. I know I certainly didn't.

I shook my head. "No, thank you, Scott. I'm good." I smiled and wondered if before now, had I ever had a conversation with Scott? Probably not. Being stuck in my own world of Abby Masters didn't leave much room for anyone else.

"Scott, are you happy here? Because if you're not, please, just fucking quit."

His brows rose in surprise... maybe shock. Scott shook his head. "I suppose you could consider me happy. I am paid to keep your garden."

"Oh Scott, it's not my garden you keep. It's my mother's."

Scott appeared to have blushed. It is hot here in Texas, but a few minutes ago, his face had not been flushed. My brow rose. "Scott, be careful with my mother. She's not who she seems to be."

"Ahh, your mother is fine, Ms. Abby." It was at this moment that Scott realized my suitcase was at my side. "Ms. Abby, are you going on a trip?"

I nodded and lowered my gaze. "Something like that. Scott?" I glanced up to find the gardener watching me. "Leave here and find something new. She doesn't deserve your kindness." Scott's mouth opened to say something but I stopped him. I held my hand up and shook my head. "Don't, just please, help yourself and leave. The moment she realizes she has no further need for you, she'll toss you away just like she did to me."

Pressing the key lock, the doors to my Audi unlocked. I opened the trunk and Scott was nice enough to lift my bag inside.

"Ms. Abby, please, don't leave like this. Your mother loves you."

I laughed and glanced at the gardener. "She has no idea what love is and it's obvious neither do you. Good day, Scott, and thank you for my bag." I closed the trunk then climbed into the front seat, closing the driver's door. I pressed the button to turn on the car and it began to purr. I glanced over at Scott, who was wearing the saddest face I've ever seen on a man. It was almost pathetic.

Leaving my home wasn't as hard as I thought it would be. My stomach was in knots though. I wasn't sure if it was from the almost panic attack or the conversation I was about to have with my father. I sighed heavily, knowing it was definitely the latter.

After twenty minutes of driving toward downtown Fort Worth, I pulled into my father's firm and stared at the building.

He was the man in charge and most days, he was here. Today, I wondered if he was working, if he was still with his secretary, or if he'd finally given up on her.

My phone in hand, I pressed the speed dial to his private line. It rang twice and he answered.

"Phil Masters."

"Daddy?" I barely whispered then cleared my throat. "Daddy?" My stomach was hurting in a pretty bad way and my chest tightened.

"Abby? Is everything all right?" There was a slight alarm in his voice. I wondered if Mama called him.

"Yes, I'm fine. I called," I swallowed hard, "to tell you I'm leaving."

"Oh, all right, darling. Let us know when you get there, okay? I'm a little busy right now." I heard a faint giggle in the background. I sighed and knew he had no idea what I was doing.

"I'm not coming back." I waited for his response. I wondered if he had even heard me. I was about to speak again when he finally spoke something.

"Right. I'm sure I'll see you at dinner tonight. Don't be reckless, Abby. It would kill your mother." Then… he hung up.

Once again, a tear streamed down my cheek. I threw my phone across my car and screamed. My mother hates me and my father doesn't even know I exist. Right. Yes. Everything is about to completely change. Starting right now.

ick up Fueled Desire to continue reading day!

ALSO BY J. MORGAN

Check out Misadventures with a Firefighter, available now!

Misadventures of a Firefighter

Cara Murphy is a New York City kindergarten teacher with a bright future and tenure on the horizon, and she won't let anything—any man—distract her. She's had her heart broken before, and she won't make that mistake twice. She's got her career to focus on, and being single has many, many advantages.

Noah Hughes is a firefighter with a charred heart who heats up every room he enters, but he lives solely for the happiness of his five-year-old son. When he crosses paths with Cara at a club, sparks fly, and they share a hot night of passion. But that flame is quickly doused during a surprise second encounter.

Continuing to see each other would truly be playing with fire, but Cara and Noah can't stop. Still, Cara's career is in jeopardy, and Noah's heart is locked in guilt. Is there really a chance they could build a love that forever burns bright?

Preorder

Misadventures with a Lawyer

Legendary lawyer Chase Newstrom is as famous in court as he is with the ladies. His work-hard, play-harder mindset is why he's never lost a case…or lacked a model on his arm. But a recent twist before the bench threatens to derail his perfect record.

Chase turns to junior associate Ainsley Speire to solve his case's problems after hours so he can gallivant around town with yet another lady friend, and Ainsley, despite being driven and focused, is none too pleased with her boss's demands. She's had to cancel long-standing plans at the last minute, again…and vows it's for the last time.

Ainsley sits down with Chase's most expensive scotch in one hand and fancy pen in the other and pours it all out, literally and figuratively. When Chase finds the note—and a passed-out Ainsley—he's intrigued. Perhaps there's more to the soft-spoken Ms. Speire than he thought.

Ainsley wakes to Chase's trademark cocky grin, and Chase sees a new spark in Ainsley's eyes. Anything between them would be an HR nightmare, but is there a chance Chase and Ainsley are willing to work together on one more case? A case that promises a lifetime sentence of love?

Read these stories in KU!

Southern Roots series

Southern Roots

City Lights

Fueled Desire

Driven Hunger

Paramour

Playing Her Body

Suspenseful Seduction World

Submitting to Paradise

Claiming His Snow

Hot SEALs

Guarded by a SEAL

Available wide!

Special Ops series

Delta Force

Sniper

Misadventures series

Misadventures with a Firefighter

Misadventures with a Lawyer

ABOUT THE AUTHOR

USA TODAY and Award-winning Bestselling Author, Julie Morgan (writing as J. Morgan), holds a degree in Computer Science and loves science fiction shows and movies. Encouraged by her family, she began writing. Originally from Texas, Julie now resides in Central Florida with her husband and daughter where she is an advocate for Special Needs children and can be found playing games with her daughter when she isn't lost in another world.

Keep up with Julie. Join her newsletter and receive a free book!
www.juliemorganbooks.com/newsletter.html
julie@juliemorganbooks.com

 facebook.com/juliemorganbook
 twitter.com/juliemorganbook
 instagram.com/JulieMorganBooks